Nowhere to Run . . .
Nowhere to Hide.

Al has had enough. He's going to pay back his sister once and for all. A stink bomb in the middle of her dumb chess club meeting should do the trick.

But when Al sets off the bomb, it doesn't smell . . . it oozes.

All over his sister's cat . . .

All over his best friend . . .

And now it's coming after Al!

Also from R. L. Stine

The Beast
The Beast 2

R. L. Stine's Ghosts of Fear Street
#1 Hide and Shriek
#2 Who's Been Sleeping in My Grave?
#3 Attack of the Aqua Apes
#4 Nightmare in 3-D
#5 Stay Away from the Tree House
#6 Eye of the Fortuneteller
#7 Fright Knight

Available from MINSTREL Books

R·L·STINE'S
GHOSTS OF FEAR STREET ®

THE OOZE

A Parachute Press Book

A MINSTREL® BOOK

PUBLISHED BY POCKET BOOKS

New York   London   Toronto   Sydney   Tokyo   Singapore

This book is a work of fiction. Names, characters, places and incidents are products of the author's imagination or are used fictitiously. Any resemblance to actual events or locales or persons, living or dead, is entirely coincidental.

A MINSTREL PAPERBACK *Original*

 A Minstrel Paperback published by
POCKET BOOKS, a division of Simon & Schuster Inc.
1230 Avenue of the Americas, New York, NY 10020

Copyright © 1996 by Parachute Press, Inc.

THE OOZE WRITTEN BY STEPHEN ROOS

All rights reserved, including the right to reproduce this book or portions thereof in any form whatsoever. For information address Pocket Books, 1230 Avenue of the Americas, New York, NY 10020

ISBN: 0-671-52948-X

First Minstrel Books printing May 1996

10 9 8 7 6 5 4 3 2 1

FEAR STREET is a registered trademark of Parachute Press, Inc.

A MINSTREL BOOK and colophon are registered trademarks of Simon & Schuster Inc.

Cover art by Mark Garro

Printed in the U.S.A.

R·L·STINE'S
GHOSTS of FEAR STREET®

THE OOZE

Most kids don't have to beg their dogs to chase a ball. But Tubby isn't like most dogs.

"Get the ball, Tubby!" I pleaded as I wound up for the throw. "You can do it!"

Tubby wagged his tail. Then he noticed it moving and tried to bite it.

"Come on, Tubby!" I shouted. I hurled the yellow tennis ball. It flew right by his face.

Tubby plopped down on the grass. He didn't even blink as the ball whizzed by.

The sliding back door slammed. I turned and saw my older sister, Michelle, walking toward me. As usual, she had a textbook tucked under her arm.

"When are you going to face reality, Al?" she asked

as she sat down under the apple tree. "Your dog is a total moron!"

"No, he isn't," I protested. "He just doesn't feel like playing now. Right, Tubby?" I dropped down next to him and patted his big head. His shaggy brown and white fur felt warm from the sun.

Michelle snorted and opened her calculus textbook.

"You're studying?" I asked. "On a Saturday? And you call Tubby stupid?"

"I want to graduate with the highest grades in my whole ninth-grade class," Michelle said.

Michelle is fourteen, just three years older than I am. But she's already doing college-level math.

If you haven't figured it out already, being smart means everything to her. And to my parents, too. The three of them are genuises. I mean it. They are really genuises.

It's a pain. Teachers are always asking me if I'm Michelle Sterner's little brother. When I say yes, they expect me to study twenty-four hours a day. The way she does.

I'm smart. Probably as smart as Michelle. But I don't want to spend my whole life with my nose in a book. I like to have fun.

All Michelle likes to do is study, study, study. If you ask me, she's too smart for her own good.

Tubby rose slowly to his feet with a big sigh. He wandered over to the hedge that runs along the side of the yard and began to dig.

2

Then he trotted over to Michelle and started a new hole there.

A few minutes later he had another hole going by the back fence.

Michelle shook her head. "Your dog is so stupid he can't even remember where he buried his bone. You should get a cat," Michelle told me. "Cats are very intelligent."

"Like Chester?" I asked. Chester is Michelle's cat. Michelle thinks he is *brilliant.*

"Did I tell you he can count up to eight now?" Michelle asked.

"Can he multiply and divide, too?" I joked.

Michelle stuck her tongue out at me. "He can snap up the window shade when he wants some light. And he knows how to jump on the electric can opener when he's hungry. And—"

"Who cares if he's smart?" I interrupted. "That's not what pets are for."

But Michelle paid no attention to me. "I saw a cat on TV that learned how to flush the toilet," she continued. "I'm teaching Chester how to do it, too."

"Boy, are you lazy, Michelle. Why can't you flush the toilet yourself?"

"He won't be flushing it for me, you jerk. I'm going to teach him how to use the bathroom—the way we do. And then we won't need kitty litter anymore!"

"Michelle, you're losing it. You're totally losing it."

"You're just jealous because you can't even teach

3

Tubby to fetch. Face it, Al. Chester is a billion times smarter than your dog. He's probably even smarter than you."

"You're a riot, Michelle. A real riot."

"If you ask Chester nicely," Michelle went on, "I'm sure he'll teach you how to flush the toilet, too!"

"Let's go inside, Tubby," I called out to my dog. "We don't need to listen to this!"

I crossed the lawn and grabbed Tubby's collar. I had to tug on it three times—hard—before he figured out I wanted him to come with me. Then we went inside.

Mom stood at the kitchen counter, icing a cake. "Don't look, Al!" she said, waving a spatula with chocolate all over it.

Little flecks of chocolate dotted Mom's face. They looked like extra-big freckles. Mom and I both have a ton of freckles, and the same red hair and brown eyes.

"But, Mom!" I exclaimed. "Today's my birthday. I already know that's my birthday cake." You don't have to be a genius to figure this one out, I thought.

"I still want it to be a surprise," she said firmly. "Go wait in your room. And don't come out until you hear us singing. You can work on memorizing all the capitals of South American countries for school."

I sighed. "I know every single one of them by heart, Mom."

"How about studying for Wednesday's Science Bowl?" Mom suggested.

I shrugged and headed down the hall to my room, dragging Tubby behind me. Around my house, if you aren't studying for one thing, you're studying for another.

Mom and Dad are research scientists. Which is how I came to be named Al, after Albert Einstein himself.

I guess I can't blame them for hoping I'd turn out to be some kind of scientific genius. But I wish they could understand that playing baseball and hanging out with my friends isn't a waste of my "wonderful brain," as my mom says.

Tubby yawned and collapsed on the floor the moment we hit my room. I reached for my copy of *Super Blades* magazine and dropped down on my bed.

I wondered what Mom and Dad had planned for my birthday this year. They always take Michelle and me to something cultural on our birthdays. Sometimes it's a concert, or if I'm really out of luck, we go to an opera.

They always give us presents that are educational, too. Boring. Totally boring.

I wanted this year to be different. So I hinted for a pair of in-line skates. And I was pretty obvious about it. I left the ads for my favorites all over the place.

Plus, I never missed a chance to mention them— making them sound real educational. I told my mom that in-line skates were excellent for eye-motor co-ordination.

I told Michelle that they improved your split-second decision-making process.

I told my dad about the big skate sale at Dalby's.

I hoped they figured it out. For three *brilliant* people, they can be pretty dense sometimes.

As I flipped through *Super Blades,* I heard footsteps stomping down the basement stairs. That meant they were almost ready to start singing. We always use the basement for celebrations.

I dropped my skating magazine on the floor and jumped off the bed. "Ready?" I yelled down the hall.

"Almost, Al!" my father called.

I was really excited. I could almost feel those in-line skates on my feet!

"Say when!" I shouted.

I couldn't stand the suspense one more second.

"Now?" I yelled.

"Now!"

I broke into a run.

I jerked open the basement door and saw Mom and Dad at the bottom of the stairs. Michelle stood in front of them, holding the cake. All the candles were lit.

They started to sing "Happy Birthday."

I walked down the steps slowly, gazing around the basement, trying to spot my present.

My eyes darted to Mom's computer station.

Nothing there.

I glanced at the big table in the middle of the room.

It had one of Michelle's experiments on top. That's all.

Then I glimpsed the solar motorboat my dad was working on. Thousands of high-tech tools surrounded it. No present.

Nothing.

I don't believe this, I thought. I'm not getting skates—I'm not getting a birthday present at all.

I had three more steps to go. I shot one last look around, but I didn't see anything with wrapping paper on it.

I finally reached the bottom of the stairs, right where Michelle and my parents stood—and got the biggest surprise of my life.

2

BOOM!

A huge explosion rocked the basement.

The floor, the walls—everything shook. Michelle's experiment soared from the table and crashed to the floor. Dad's tools flew everywhere.

I screamed as the force of the blast knocked me down. I landed with a thud on the hard cement.

Mom, Dad, and Michelle hovered over me. Laughing. Laughing their heads off.

"You aren't hurt, are you, Al?" Mom asked, still chuckling.

"I'm okay," I grumbled. "What's going on? What's so funny?"

"Surprise!" Dad sang out. "We wanted to celebrate your birthday with a big bang!"

"Uh, great," I said, brushing myself off.

"He doesn't get it," Michelle announced.

"Get what?" I hated to admit it, but I really was confused.

"We're giving you a chemistry set!" Mom explained. She stepped aside. Behind her, on the floor, sat a huge box—with the words *Future Scientist* printed in big red letters across the front.

"Welcome to the wonderful world of chemistry, Al," Dad said. "You're going to have all sorts of exciting adventures with this set!"

He glanced down at the broken glass and spilled chemicals on the floor. "Michelle had to borrow a few things from your set to make the bang. Don't worry. We'll replace everything."

"Thanks a lot, Mom. Dad," I mumbled. "The chemistry set is so . . ."

"So stimulating?" Dad asked.

"That's exactly the word I was looking for," I said.

"Do you *really* like it, Al?" Mom asked.

"I love it, Mom," I lied.

I didn't want to hurt their feelings. I could see that they thought the chemistry set was an incredible present.

I told you they could be dense.

Trying hard to hide my disappointment, I opened

the box and checked out the rack of test tubes inside. But when I picked up a tube with green liquid inside, Dad grabbed it from me.

"Not yet, Al," he said, placing the tube back in the rack.

"Why not?" I asked.

"You need a lesson in how to handle all these chemicals," Mom said.

"Remember, this isn't a toy," Dad added. "Michelle will teach you how to use the chemistry set safely."

"Why not you or Mom?" I asked.

"Oh, it's been a long time since your mother or I handled a chemistry set," Dad replied. "And Michelle's more up on things than we ever were."

"It was Michelle who made the bang," Mom added. "It was her way of saying happy birthday."

Somehow that didn't surprise me.

"Just tell Michelle when you want to start using it," Mom went on.

"I can't wait," I answered, hoping I sounded as though I meant it. "I really can't wait."

If I had known I was about to enter the worst nightmare you could imagine, I would never have opened that box.

I would have waited forever!

3

What a birthday.

First a chemistry set. Then a night at the opera—that I thought would never end.

Even when the villain finally stabbed the hero through the heart, the guy kept on singing and singing.

And today—the day after my birthday—wasn't turning out much better.

It was Sunday. To me, that meant I should be outside doing something fun. To Mom and Dad, it meant studying. So that's what I was doing—memorizing facts from my *Science Teasers* book for the Science Bowl.

Shadyside Middle School has won the state championship three years in a row. With Michelle on the team, how could they lose?

But last year Michelle went on to Shadyside High. Now everyone says it's my turn to keep up the school's winning tradition! Which is why I'm stuck in my room, studying away.

I read the first question—what is the end product of photosynthesis?

Before I could come up with the answer, I smelled something unbelievably putrid in the house. I had to investigate. People died from smells that bad!

I checked all the bedrooms as I made my way down the hall. They were empty.

As soon as I spotted Michelle in the kitchen, I knew I had found the source of the foul odor.

"You're baking brownies again, aren't you?" I accused her. "Admit it, Michelle!"

"Don't touch them!" she snarled, stepping in front of the counter, blocking them from view. "Don't even look at them!"

"Too late," I told her. "I already saw them. They're burnt to a crisp!"

"They're just a little brown around the edges," she declared. "My chess club will love them."

"You're going to poison your friends?" I asked. "Even for you, that's low."

Someone knocked at the door, and Michelle sprang

for it. But I got there first. Colin, my best friend, stepped inside.

"Oh, it's just you," Michelle muttered.

"Whoa!" Colin said. "What's wrong with *just me?*"

"Her chess club is having a meeting here," I explained. "She was probably hoping you were Jonathan Muller. He's the president of the club, and she has a total crush on him."

"I do not!" Michelle snapped. But her face turned bright red.

"Yeah, right," I answered. "You should see her looseleaf binder." I grinned at Colin. "She has entire pages with 'Michelle Sterner-Muller' written all over them. She wants to marry the guy or something."

Colin snickered. Michelle threw a potholder at me. "What were you doing snooping in my binder?" she shrieked. "That's my personal property!"

I threw the potholder back at her. "Mom said I could," I informed her, "because I ran out of looseleaf paper."

Michelle glared at me. "If you tell anyone, I'll kill you." She turned to Colin. "You, too," she threatened.

"It's cool," Colin said. "Can I have a brownie?"

Before I could stop him, Colin popped a killer brownie into his mouth.

"Excuse me while I dial the paramedics," I said.

"Hey, they're unbelievable!" Colin exclaimed.

"See?" Michelle replied proudly.

"They are totally unbelievable." Colin swallowed. "How do you get them to taste like charcoal?"

I gave Colin a high five. "Score!" he yelled. "Two points!"

"Get out of here, you idiots!" Michelle screamed.

"Come on, Colin," I said. "Let's go down to the basement. I want to show you my birthday present."

"Oh, yeah! I can't wait to see the skates," Colin answered.

I shook my head. "Didn't get them."

"No way!" Colin exclaimed. "Your parents did it to you again?"

"Yep." What else was there to say?

I led Colin downstairs. Chester, Michelle's *brilliant* cat, followed us. He curled up in a corner and watched as we opened the chemistry set. Watched with a look that seemed to say "I'm telling Michelle. I'm telling Michelle. You're not supposed to touch that without Michelle."

It's a good thing my sister hasn't taught him to talk yet, I thought.

Colin pulled out a test tube filled with purple crystals. "What are you supposed to do with all this stuff?"

"I don't know yet. I'm not supposed to use it until Michelle shows me how," I answered.

I heard the doorbell ring. Michelle's chess geeks were here.

"We don't have to wait for her." Colin grinned.

14

"Let's have some fun with it on our own." He reached for a test tube filled with red liquid and emptied it into a beaker.

"Better not," I warned him. "You can get into real trouble if you don't know what you're doing."

"I'm not planning anything major," Colin said. "Just a little stink bomb."

"I don't know," I said. "My mom and dad told me not "

"We can set it off upstairs," Colin interrupted. "Don't you want to see your sister choking and gagging—right in front of that guy she likes?"

That *would* be pretty funny. At least until my parents found out.

"Where's the manual?" Colin asked, digging through the box.

"I thought you knew how to make one!" I replied.

"No. No, I don't," Colin admitted. "But the instructions must be in here somewhere.

"Oh, sure," I said sarcastically. "Just look under *S* for *stink.*"

Colin found the instruction booklet and flipped through it, shaking his head. "Nothing here," he muttered.

"Come on," I said. "Let's go out. We can go to the mall or something."

"No. Let's stay here. We don't need instructions. It can't be *that* hard to make a bad smell," Colin declared. "Your sister does it without even trying."

I laughed. Colin can always make me laugh. That's one of the reasons we're best friends.

Colin tipped the test tube of purple crystals over the red liquid.

"Colin. Don't do it," I warned.

He ignored me.

He tipped the test tube some more.

"Colin! You don't know what you're doing!" I yelled.

The purple crystals began to tumble out.

I looked at the labels on the test tubes. "Not the red and the purple, Colin! Not those two!" I screamed. "You'll blow up the house!"

4

I snatched up the beaker.

The purple crystals spilled from the test tube and scattered all over the worktable.

"You can't mix chemicals without knowing what will happen, Colin! Those two could have caused an explosion!" I yelled.

"Oh," Colin replied. "Does that mean no stink bomb—just because you're scared of blowing up the house?"

I laughed. I couldn't help it. Like I said, Colin knows how to crack me up.

"Okay, okay. No stink bomb." Colin gave in. "Let's go to the mall."

We started to pack up the chemistry set. "Hey!

17

What's this?" Colin asked as he tried to shove the test tube rack back into the carton.

He pulled out a single sheet of paper from the bottom of the carton. "Ha! Is this good enough for you?" he exclaimed.

I peered over his shoulder and read the paper. Directions—directions for how to make a stink bomb. Weird.

The instructions were handwritten on a bright orange piece of paper—nothing like the plain white paper the manual was printed on. Very weird.

"Let's do it," Colin urged. "We have all the stuff."

"Well, okay," I finally agreed. How could I pass up the chance to embarrass Michelle?

We measured the chemicals carefully and combined them in a clean beaker. "We'll leave this one out until we're in position upstairs," I told Colin. I showed him a test tube filled with yellow powder.

"Good idea," he answered.

We tiptoed up the stairs and into the kitchen. I peeked into the living room. Jonathan Muller stood by the fireplace, talking about some chess tournament they were organizing.

I spotted Michelle on the sofa. She leaned forward, gazing at Jonathan across the room. The other kids were all focused on Jonathan, too. Perfect.

"Come on," I whispered. I got down on my hands and knees and crawled into the living room. Crawled to the back of the couch and hid behind it. Colin followed.

"Ready?" Colin mouthed, holding out the beaker.

"Yes," I whispered, holding up the test tube. "Hold your breath."

"Don't you mean your *nose?*" Colin snickered.

I snickered, too. Then I poured the yellow powder into the beaker.

We scrunched farther down behind the couch and waited. But nothing happened.

"Take a whiff," I whispered.

Colin put the tube up to his nose. "It doesn't smell at all." He sighed.

"You jerks! What are you doing back there?" Michelle leaned over the back of the sofa, looking meaner than usual. "What is in that beaker, Al?" she demanded.

"It's nothing," I lied. "Honest!"

"You're not supposed to use your chemistry set until *I* show you how," she snapped. "Don't you ever follow directions?"

"But we did follow the directions!" Colin exclaimed, holding up the orange paper. "It's not our fault the stink bomb didn't go off!"

Thanks, Colin, I thought. Thanks a lot.

"You were trying to stink bomb my meeting?" Michelle screeched. "Wait till I tell Mom and Dad. Just wait."

Colin and I took off into the kitchen.

"And leave that chemistry set alone," Michelle called after us.

"Your little brother can't even figure out how to make a stink bomb?" I heard someone say to Michelle. "Are you sure you two are related?"

I felt like a total jerk. Getting caught using the chemistry set was bad enough. But it was worse knowing Michelle and her friends thought I was too dumb to make a stink bomb.

"What should we do with this gunk?" Colin asked when we returned to the basement.

"Throw it out, I guess."

"In the garbage?" Colin asked.

"No, I'll pour it down the sink." I reached for the beaker and noticed that the solution was turning a funny orange color. Neon orange.

"It's working *now?*" Colin groaned.

I smelled the gloppy mess. "No. No, it's not working. It still doesn't stink," I told him.

I placed the beaker on the table. "Let's put the chemistry set away, before my mom gets home. She'll go ballistic if she knows I fooled around with it— without Michelle's help."

"Why bother?" Colin asked. "Michelle's going to tell on you anyway. You know she will."

He had a point. She probably would.

Chester still sat in the corner of the basement. I had forgotten he was even there. He let out a long meow. Then stood up—and leaped onto the table.

He strolled toward the beaker, his tail flicking back and forth.

"Shouldn't you be doing your math problems, Chester?" I asked. Chester padded closer to the beaker.

"Off the table. Off!" I gave the cat a little push— and knocked over the stink bomb.

The orange goo poured out. It oozed across the table. Thick and slimy.

Some of it slid over one of Chester's front paws.

All his hair stood straight up.

He arched his back. Flattened his ears.

He hissed at the gooey stuff, baring his sharp white teeth.

Then he leaped off the table, raced up the stairs, and cowered near the door.

"Look at it!" Colin said, amazed. "It's oozing everywhere."

Colin was right. The stuff had oozed across the table. Down the table legs. Onto the floor.

Now it started oozing across the room.

"My mom will kill me if we don't have this stuff cleaned up by the time she gets home!"

I hurried over to the sink and pulled out a big roll of paper towels. I ripped off a long sheet and handed it to Colin.

"Don't get any of it on you," I instructed. "I don't know what these chemicals do to skin."

Colin wrapped the paper towels around his left

hand until it was covered with a wad as big as a catcher's mitt.

Then we went after the ooze.

It didn't soak into the paper towels the way I expected it to. Every time I touched it, it broke into little balls and rolled away.

"This stuff is weird!" Colin exclaimed. "Really weird!"

"Try it like this," I suggested. With a paper towel in each hand, I trapped some ooze between them. Even through the toweling the stuff felt spongy and squishy.

"I'll finish the table. You wipe up the floor," I ordered as I captured another neon-orange glob.

"We're never going to clean up all this gunk! It keeps running away!" Colin made another paper towel catcher's mitt. He crawled across the floor. Trying to wipe up the runny goop.

"We have to," I told him. "We have to clean it up. No way Mom can see this mess. No way!" I opened up a second roll of paper towels and started a fresh attack on the ooze.

We chased the stuff around the room until there was only one puddle left—on the table. It slid away as soon as the paper towel touched it. But I had my other hand ready to stop it.

"Done!" Colin cried. "What should we do with all the paper towels? Flush them?"

I stared at the floor. At the mountain of paper towels heaped there.

"No. No. We can't do that. They'll clog up the toilet," I answered.

"Okay," Colin replied. "I'll just throw them in the garbage."

"No. No. We can't do that, either. They don't pick up garbage until Thursday," I explained. "I don't want any sign of this stuff around."

My eyes searched the basement. I spotted a big red chest—an old cooler that Dad used when he went fishing. Perfect.

"We'll stuff them in here," I said. "And we'd better hurry. Mom will be home any second."

I lifted the top of the chest. It was filled with kitty litter. Bags and bags of kitty litter.

"Al? Are you down there? Al?" Mom called from the top of the basement steps. "I'm home!"

5

"**H**elp me, Colin!" I whispered as I started tossing the bags out.

Click. Click. Click.

The sound of Mom's high-heeled shoes clicked down the basement steps.

"Hurry, Colin. Hurry!"

I gathered up huge bunches of paper towels, careful not to get any of the ooze on my hands.

Chester yowled. "What's wrong, kitty cat?" Mom said on the way down. "It's just me. Nothing to be afraid of."

Mom's heels clicked down the stairs louder—closer.

I yanked the lid off the cooler and crammed the

paper towels inside. Colin shoved his on top and slammed on the lid.

We did it! With my left foot I kicked the cooler under the table—just as Mom stepped into the room. "Having fun?" she asked.

"Just hanging out," I answered, trying to sound normal.

Mom studied me suspiciously. "I see you have the chemistry set out. Did Michelle give you the safety lesson yet, Al?"

"Not yet. But she will," I said. "When the chess club leaves."

Oh, no! I noticed a big drop of the ooze on the worktable. I leaned against the table—trying to look casual. I placed my right hand on top of the orange glob.

"I really don't want you using the chemistry set until you know all the safety rules," Mom warned.

Good. She didn't notice the ooze. "Honest, Mom," I answered. "We were just looking at the test tubes."

I could feel the ooze under my palm. It was growing warm. And it started to slide up between my fingers.

"Okay. If you boys want a snack, there's still plenty of birthday cake left," Mom told us.

The ooze seeped out some more. I slammed my left hand down on top of my right one to cover it. I wasn't going to be able to hide the gooey stuff much longer.

"Awesome, Mrs. Sterner," Colin said. "We will most definitely come up for some cake later."

The ooze started to crawl up through my left hand now. Go, I silently begged my mom. Go upstairs.

"All right," Mom said, and headed back up to the kitchen.

I didn't move until I heard the basement door shut behind her. Then I peered down at my hands. The ooze covered both my palms. And it was spreading up onto my wrists.

"Help me get this gunk off!" I told Colin.

"That stuff is gross," Colin complained. But he made another towel mitt and wiped and wiped—cleaning away the last sign of the weird slimy goo.

When I woke up the next morning, I felt really tired. As if I hadn't slept at all.

I forced myself to sit up. Clothes. What clothes should I wear to school? I couldn't decide. Finally I pulled on a pair of jeans and the first shirt I found when I reached into the closet.

Now I needed socks and shoes. Mom just did the laundry, I remembered. So where did she put my socks?

Forget it, I told myself. I was already running late. The socks I wore yesterday weren't *too* dirty. And they were in my shoes, so I didn't have to hunt all over for them.

I sat down on the bed and pulled on my socks. Then I reached down for a shoe.

I held it for a while, just staring at it. What was

wrong with me this morning? Why was I moving so slowly?

I stuffed my foot into the shoe. It felt kind of weird. It didn't hurt exactly. It just felt weird.

"Al, hurry up," Mom called.

I shoved on my other shoe and hurried down the hall. As I walked through the kitchen door, I tripped.

Of course, Michelle didn't miss that one! She laughed so hard she almost choked on her granola.

I looked down to see what I had tripped over, but there was nothing there.

"You idiot!" Michelle laughed as she wiped the tears from her eyes.

"Al could have hurt himself, Michelle!" Mom scolded.

"That's right, Michelle," Dad added. "It's not polite to laugh."

"But his shoes! Look at his shoes!"

"These are the shoes I always wear," I said. "What's wrong with them?"

Dad snorted. I could tell he was trying not to laugh now.

"Oh, my gosh!" Mom exclaimed. "Michelle's right!"

I looked down at my shoes—and gasped!

6

My left shoe was on my right foot!

And my right shoe was on . . . well, I guess you can figure the rest out for yourself.

"No wonder they felt weird," I mumbled. I couldn't believe I had put my shoes on the wrong feet. I must really be tired, I thought.

Feeling a little stupid, I kicked off my shoes and put them on the right feet.

"When are you going to learn to dress yourself, Al?" Michelle teased.

"Now, Michelle," Dad said. "Your brother has been dressing himself since—"

"Since he was ten," Michelle hooted.

"Since he was two," Dad finished.

"Maybe Al better check out summer school—a Getting Dressed for Beginners class," Michelle suggested, still not letting up.

"Has Chester learned any new tricks?" Dad asked, changing the subject to get Michelle off my back. Michelle could talk all day about how smart her cat was.

Chester was snoozing by the stove. "Come here, Chester," Michelle called. "Show Dad how you can add. What is one and one?"

Chester jumped into Michelle's lap and collapsed. "Come on, Chester!" Michelle coaxed. "One and one."

Chester didn't move.

"I'll get a can of cat food," Dad suggested. "That will get him thinking."

Dad slid the can into the electric can opener. "Come on, Chester," he said. "Jump on the lever!"

Chester didn't move.

"I wonder if something is wrong with him." Michelle sounded worried.

"He probably isn't hungry." Dad tried to make her feel better.

Chester might not be hungry. But I was. Hungry and late.

I shoveled down some oatmeal and a piece of toast. Then I grabbed my backpack and headed out the door. "Bye!" I yelled on my way out.

We live only two blocks from Shadyside Middle

School. I ran all the way there and made it before the bell rang.

A girl with curly red hair raced up the front steps ahead of me.

"Hey, Al!" I shouted.

She looked over her shoulder. "Hey, Al!" she shouted back at me.

I'm Albert, of course, and her name is Alix. But we kid around, pretending we have the same name. This year we were going to be partners in the Science Bowl.

"You know when Louis Pasteur was born?" I asked.

"1822," she shot back at me. "You know what elements are in water?"

I said the first thing that popped into my head. "Peanut butter and jelly."

She laughed.

"So do you think we'll win?" I asked her.

"Are you kidding?" Alix grinned. "We're the team to beat! No sweat!"

We ran down the hall together and made it to class just as the bell rang.

"Oooh, Al-vin. You almost got a tardy slip," Eric Rice whispered.

He likes to call me Alvin because he thinks it makes me mad. He's a total jerk.

But he's also the toughest kid in the sixth grade. And he sits right behind me. So I try not to get into any arguments with him.

"Who did their memorization?" Miss Scott, our teacher, asked.

All the kids raised their hands. Even Eric. As if he ever does his homework!

I raised my hand, too. Then I realized I couldn't remember what we were supposed to have memorized.

"Who can tell me what the capital of Peru is?" Miss Scott asked, glancing around the class.

As usual Toad waved his hand the hardest. We all called him Toad—even the teachers. But no one could remember how his nickname got started. He was on one of the Science Bowl teams Alix and I would be competing against.

A fly landed on my desk. I watched it rub its front legs over its head again and again.

"How about you, Melanie?" Miss Scott asked.

"It's Lima, isn't it?" Melanie answered.

"Are you asking me or telling me?" Miss Scott replied.

"Well, maybe a little of both," Melanie admitted.

To that fly, I bet my desk is like a huge desert, I thought. I wished I had a little crumb to give it.

"Well, you are right," Miss Scott said. "The capital of Peru is Lima."

"Boy, did she ever luck out," Eric muttered.

Huh? I hadn't really been paying attention.

"Eric?" Miss Scott asked. "Did you have something to add?"

"No, Miss Scott," Eric answered.

"Well, maybe you can tell us the capital of Brazil," Miss Scott said.

There was a pause. We all waited for Eric to say something.

I peered out the window—and noticed some little kids playing dodgeball outside. I used to love to play dodgeball.

"The capital of Brazil, Eric," Miss Scott repeated.

"Now?" Eric asked. "You mean like right now?"

"Well, soon, Eric," Miss Scott said. "The school year ends in June!"

Everyone in the class laughed.

Except Eric, of course.

I kept staring out the window again. That kid in the yellow sweater is going to get creamed, I thought. He is way too slow for dodgeball.

"Eric, the capital of Brazil, please."

"Well, let's see," Eric said slowly.

"You did memorize the capitals over the weekend, didn't you?"

"Oh, sure," Eric said. "Could you repeat the name of the country, please?"

The kids laughed harder.

"Eric, if you didn't study over the weekend, I'll have to ask you to stay after school today," Miss Scott said.

"I have baseball this afternoon," Eric said. "You can't keep me after school today."

Baseball is a good game, too, I thought. Which do I like better—dodgeball or baseball?

"Schoolwork before baseball," Miss Scott declared. "You know the rules, Eric."

There was a knock at the door. Mr. Emerson, the principal, stood in the doorway.

"Excuse me, class," Miss Scott said. "I'll be back in a minute." As soon as Miss Scott joined Mr. Emerson in the hall, Eric turned to me.

"Okay, Al, what's the answer?" he demanded.

"Huh? Answer to what?"

"The capital of Brazil, you jerk," Eric said. "Weren't you listening?"

"Do you think there's going to be another baseball strike?" I asked.

"Come on, Sterner!" Eric hissed. "What is the capital of Brazil?"

"Hot dogs," I said.

"What are you talking about?" Eric demanded.

"I was just thinking that hot dogs taste better at the ballpark than anywhere else. Do you know why?" I asked.

"Tell me the capital of Brazil! Now!" Eric said. I noticed a little vein throbbing in his forehead.

"Oh, it's Cleveland," I whispered just as Miss Scott came back into the classroom.

"Eric?" Miss Scott asked. "What is the capital of Brazil?"

"Cleveland," Eric announced.

The whole class laughed. Even Miss Scott had trouble keeping a straight face.

Cleveland? I thought. Why did I say Cleveland?

"Eric," Miss Scott said, "you should plan on staying after school. I see we have our work cut out for us!"

"Cleveland isn't the capital of Brazil?" Eric asked slowly.

"Cleveland is in Ohio," Miss Scott replied. "And it isn't even the capital there!"

I felt Eric's hot breath against my ear. "I'm going to get you for that, Sterner," Eric whispered. "I'm going to get you!"

7

The minute the last bell rang, I jumped out of my chair and raced out the door.

I knew Miss Scott was keeping Eric after school. But I wasn't taking any chances. I wanted to be home—with the door locked—before he even left the building.

I ran down the hall, out the front door, and down the steps. And I kept on running.

I kept hearing Eric's voice in my head. *I'm going to get you for that, Sterner. I'm going to get you.*

And I knew he would.

During math class he passed me a note. A note that mentioned specific bones of my body—and what he planned to do to them.

I thought about the note—and ran faster. I ran three blocks. Four blocks. Five.

My lungs were burning. My legs were aching. But I knew I would feel a lot worse if Eric caught me.

I ran another block—and hit a red light. I glanced behind me as I waited for the light to change.

No Eric yet.

The moment the light turned green I sprinted across the street. Then I stopped.

Wait. There is no stoplight on my way home from school.

I stared around. And I didn't recognize anything. Not anything.

That's impossible, I thought. I have lived in Shadyside my whole life. I should recognize something.

I looked up at the street sign. "Fear Street."

I knew that name. Everybody in Shadyside knew Fear Street. But I couldn't remember ever being on the street before.

I passed house after house. Some were big and fancy. Some were small and run-down. But none of them looked familiar.

Don't panic, I ordered myself. You can't be more than a couple of blocks away from home.

I studied both directions. Which way should I go? If I went the wrong way I might run straight into Eric.

I began to run again. I didn't know where I was headed. But it felt safer to keep running.

Four blocks. Five blocks. Six. Seven. Eight. I ran until there were no more houses—until I hit a dead end.

I could either turn back. Or go into the Fear Street Woods. If I turned back, I might run into Eric, I reasoned.

So I chose the woods. He'd never find me there.

I darted between the trees. They were tall and close together. Hardly any light filtered through their leafy branches. The deeper I walked into the woods, the darker it got.

And it was also getting late. Eric had probably left school by now, I realized.

I heard a rustling sound in the trees behind me. *Oh, no!* I thought. *It's Eric. He found me. I'm dead meat.*

I charged through the trees—and lost my balance. My feet slid out from under me.

I flew through the air, into a clearing, and—splash! I landed up to my knees in water. In a lake—the Fear Street lake.

My shoes were soaked. My feet were freezing.

I sloshed my way up the bank. Climbed out of the water quickly. I had to keep running—no matter how wet my shoes were. No matter how cold my feet felt. No matter what! Because if Eric caught me, he was going to pound me into the ground.

I heard footsteps.

I ran faster and faster, but the footsteps were gaining on me. I pumped my legs as hard as I could. My shoes squished as I ran.

But Eric was too fast.

He grabbed my shoulders from behind—and whirled me around.

8

"**H**ey, where are you going?"

It wasn't Eric! It was Colin!

"Colin, you have to help me!" I cried. "I'm totally lost, and I have to get home before Eric finds me."

Colin gave me a funny look. "We can almost see your house from here." He turned me around and pointed.

He was right. I could see Village Road from where we were standing. I lived on Village Road.

I felt like such an idiot. How could I get lost practically in my own backyard?

"Thanks," I mumbled to Colin. "What are you doing here, anyway?"

"I saw you take off after school. I tried to catch up,

but you were too fast. Didn't you hear me calling you?"

"No," I admitted. "I guess I was concentrating on getting away—before Eric found me."

We headed toward my house, not bothering to talk. "You want to come in?" I asked when we reached my front door.

"I can't," he said. "I have to get home. My brother and I are making a music video with my dad's new camcorder. See you tomorrow in school." He started home.

"Okay. Bye," I called. Then I hurried inside—safe from Eric.

I found Michelle sitting at the kitchen table. Her calculus textbook was open in front of her, but she wasn't reading it. She was staring off into space.

"There's something wrong with Chester," Michelle announced. "He's just not himself. He doesn't remember how to use the electric can opener. And he waits for me to turn the TV on for him."

"So what? Maybe he's just lazy," I told her.

"No, Al," she shot back. "You don't get it! There's something really wrong with him. He doesn't know what day of the week it is. He's forgotten how to tell time. He can't even count anymore!" she wailed. "Something happened to him yesterday. I know it. I just know it."

"What makes you think that?" I asked.

"Because he was fine before yesterday," she replied.

I bet no one else in the whole school—maybe even on the whole planet—has a sister who worries about her cat the way she does.

Michelle stared off into space again. Trying to figure out what was wrong with Chester.

"Hey, Tubby!" I yelled. "I'm home. Here, Tubs!" I heard Tubby race down the hall—and into the living room.

"Tubby, I'm in here. In the kitchen," I called.

Tubby woofed.

"Come on, Tubby!"

Tubby woofed again.

"Your dog is so dumb, he can't even make it from the living room to the kitchen without getting lost," Michelle said.

"Yes, he can." I picked up his bowl, poured some dog chow in, and shook the bowl back and forth.

Tubby bounded right into the kitchen. "See?" I said.

"Big deal. He can find his food bowl. Even a goldfish with a teeny, tiny brain can find its food," Michelle cracked.

"Come on, Tubby. We don't have to listen to this. Let's go outside." I marched toward the sliding back door—and walked straight into the glass.

Tubby plowed into it right beside me.

I hope Michelle didn't notice that, I thought.

"Uh, Al," Michelle said.

She noticed.

"Just a suggestion. You might try *opening* the door first next time."

"Ha, ha," I muttered.

"You're getting as dumb as Chester!" she exclaimed. "Quick, Al—how much is one and one?"

I didn't bother to answer. I opened the door and pulled Tubby out into the backyard with me.

I flopped down on the grass. Tubby flopped down beside me.

Something Michelle said bothered me. It wasn't that she called me and Tubby stupid. She does that all the time.

No, it was something she said about her cat. It triggered something in my head. Something I had to figure out—but it wasn't coming to me.

Chester was getting dumb. Is that what she said? No, she said I was getting as dumb as Chester. Were Chester and I getting dumb together?

Something was missing. It was like a jigsaw puzzle, but I couldn't find the next piece. Something happened to Chester yesterday. Hadn't Michelle said that?

Was yesterday my birthday? What happened on my birthday? The opera? No, that wasn't yesterday. No, my birthday was the day before yesterday. Wasn't it? Something happened after my birthday.

Was that yesterday? I remembered smelling something horrible—Michelle's brownies. That must be it!

Michelle's brownies were so bad they did something to my brain.

But wait. I didn't eat a brownie. Chester didn't eat a brownie. Colin ate a brownie. Only he isn't dumber than before. At least I didn't think so.

Focus, I told myself. Focus.

Colin said the brownies stank. No, he didn't! He wanted to make a stink bomb!

Did the stink bomb make me dumb? How could it? It didn't go off! It was a total disaster. It just made a lot of weird orange ooze!

All this thinking was making my head hurt. I felt as though my brain were turning into ooze.

Ooze.

Orange ooze.

What I got all over my hands.

What Chester got all over his paw.

Wait. That's it! Chester and I were getting dumber together. He touched the ooze and now he can't count. I touched the ooze and now I think Cleveland is in Brazil.

The ooze was making us stupid!

I have to talk to Colin, I decided. To run this by him. It seemed to make sense—but I wasn't sure.

I went back inside—without bumping into the glass this time. I ran to my parents' room to use the phone in there. I didn't want Michelle to overhear my conversation.

It took me three tries to get Colin's phone number right. "It's the ooze," I said when he answered.

"What?" Colin asked.

"The ooze," I repeated. Why couldn't he understand me? "The ooze is making me stupid."

"Whoa!" Colin exclaimed. "Who said you're stupid? You're not stupid."

"Yes, I am. I'm stupid—I think."

"Well, you really sound stupid now," Colin said.

"I do?" Boy was I relieved. At least I had something right. "Listen," I told Colin, "Chester stepped into the ooze with his paw. And I touched it with my hand."

"So?" Colin asked.

"So now Chester's as dumb as Tubby. And I got lost on my way home from school. And I walked into a glass door. And I couldn't even remember your telephone number. I'm stupid, Colin! I'm stupid! Chester and I are getting dumb together. And it's all because of the ooze!"

"How could some orange glop do *that?*" Colin asked.

"I don't know! How could I know? It's making me stupid!"

"Okay, okay." Colin tried to calm me down. "I have an idea. Go downstairs and look inside the cooler. Look at the ooze. You'll see. The ooze is just . . . ooze. It can't do anything to you."

"What if it can?" I asked. "What if—"

44

"Just do it," Colin told me.

I hung up and headed for the basement. Colin was right. I had to look at the ooze. See that it was just harmless glop. It was the only thing that would make me feel better.

I opened the basement door and slowly walked down the steps. I spotted the cooler under the table—exactly where I had shoved it.

I raised the lid of the cooler about an inch—and inhaled sharply.

A giant glob of ooze sat on top of the paper towels.

It was as if all the little balls that we had wiped up joined together. Joined into one huge mass of ooze.

And now it was glowing.

I opened the lid a little more—and saw that the glob had veins. *Veins!* Glowing, throbbing veins!

I started to slam the lid down—when the lump of ooze began to bubble. A small bubble broke the surface and popped. Then another. And another.

Bubble. Pop. Bubble. Pop.

More and more tiny bubbles rose to the surface and popped.

Then, without warning, a huge bubble rose up to the surface. It flipped the cooler lid wide open.

I leaped back—back from the growing bubble. But it was too late.

9

Splat!

The giant bubble burst.

A huge glob of the ooze hit my face.

It dripped down my eyes, my nose, my cheeks. It dangled from my chin in a gooey mess.

"Oh, no," I moaned. I was going to be really stupid now.

I had to wash off this horrible stuff right away! Before it made me a total moron.

I scrambled over to the cabinet under the sink. No more paper towels. We used them all yesterday.

I yanked off my T-shirt and started scrubbing my face with it. The ooze was growing warm now. Warm and extra-sticky. I couldn't get it off.

I scrubbed and scrubbed, pressing my lips together tightly. Who knew what would happen if I swallowed some? I certainly didn't—and I didn't want to find out.

My face burned and tingled as I rubbed. But I rubbed furiously until I wiped it all off.

I shoved my T-shirt into the cooler and slammed the lid on. Then I pounded up the basement stairs and down the hall to the bathroom I shared with Michelle. I had to look in the mirror—to make sure not one drop remained.

I locked the bathroom door behind me. Then I leaned as close to the mirror as I could. Searching for even a speck of the orange goo.

I didn't see any. Not a drop. But what if some had seeped into one of my ears—deep inside where I couldn't see it?

I pictured the slimy stuff sliding through my ear—and into my brain! I was doomed.

I have to tell Mom and Dad, I realized. This was a serious problem.

I knew they were going to be angry. I didn't even want to think about what they would do to me. I would probably be grounded until I finished college—if I went to college. I might be way too stupid by then to go.

I had no choice. I had to tell them. I needed their help. They were smart. They did research. Maybe they could figure out a way to save me from a lifetime of stupidity.

My stomach flip-flopped as I headed to the living room to find my parents. They were both sitting on the sofa—reading scientific journals.

I took a deep breath. "Mom, Dad, I have to talk to you," I said. My voice shook only a little.

"What's wrong, dear?" Mom asked. "You look upset."

"It's about the ooze," I started. "Chester and I both touched it. That's why—"

Dad put down his copy of *Biology Today.* "Ooze?" he asked. "What on earth is ooze?"

"Chester stepped in it," I said. "Some of it spilled on the basement table, too. That's how I touched it."

Mom and Dad glanced at each other. I could tell they were confused.

I knew I wasn't explaining things right. But I was confused, too. It was getting hard to keep everything straight in my mind.

"Where did this ooze come from?" Mom asked.

I hesitated. Tell them, I ordered myself. You have to tell them. They are the only ones who can help you.

I opened my mouth to answer—and the doorbell rang.

"I'll get it!" Michelle yelled from the kitchen.

I started to speak again—but Michelle let out a high squeal.

Mom jumped up. "What is it?" she cried. "What is it?"

Michelle practically skipped into the living room. "It's a registered letter from the Eastland Technological Institute!"

I didn't have to ask what that meant. Eastland Technologies has an annual science contest every year for high school students all over the country. You have to be a total brain even to enter. So, of course, Michelle did.

She ripped open the letter. Mom and Dad crowded behind her. Reading over her shoulder.

"You won, honey!" Mom exclaimed. "You won!"

"First prize!" Dad crowed. "We're so proud of you!"

"Mom! Dad!" I pleaded. "I need to talk to you about the ooze! Right now."

"Aren't you going to congratulate your sister?" Mom asked as she reread Michelle's letter.

"Congratulations," I muttered. Michelle didn't bother to answer. "I'm trying to tell you something important," I insisted. "You have to listen. The ooze is why Chester and I have been acting so weird."

"Do you know what I think?" Dad asked.

Yes! I thought. Dad is going to help me!

"What's that, dear?" Mom asked.

"I think we should celebrate," Dad announced. "Let's go someplace really fancy for dinner. It's Michelle's big night."

Thanks a lot, Dad, I thought.

I pulled on Mom's arm. "This is a matter of life and death!" I wailed. "I was playing with the chemistry set and—"

Mom and Dad both turned toward me.

"You played with the chemistry set?" Mom demanded.

"Before Michelle gave you the safety lesson?" Dad added.

I nodded slowly. "And now the ooze is in the cooler and it—"

Mom turned to Dad. "Let's not spoil the celebration for Michelle," she said.

"We'll talk about this tomorrow," Dad told me.

"But I could be so much dumber by then," I protested.

"Dumber? Dumber than using the chemistry set without permission? I don't think so," Mom snapped.

"Get your coat, Michelle," Dad said. "Al, we'll talk about this tomorrow."

I sighed.

Well, maybe going to a restaurant would at least help me get my mind off the ooze. After all, eating was one thing I still knew how to do.

"I'll be right there," I said. "I left my coat in my room."

"Al," Dad called after me, "It's the Science Bowl day after tomorrow."

"Yeah, Dad," I said wearily.

50

"Do you know how Michelle won her Science Bowls?" Dad asked. "By working hard. By making sacrifices."

Michelle came back with her coat and stood next to Dad. Smirking at me. She was loving every second of this.

"Maybe you should stay home," Dad continued. "You will have the house to yourself—the perfect environment for a good study session."

"But I have to eat, don't I?" I asked.

"You can heat something up in the microwave," Mom said.

"But, Mom . . ." I stopped and shook my head. Nothing I said would make them change their minds. I could see that.

"Have a good time," I muttered as they trooped out the door.

I flopped down on the couch. Now what was I supposed to do? It was clear Mom and Dad weren't going to help me.

Chester strolled into the living room. He jumped up on my lap and started to purr. He liked me a lot more now that he was stupid.

I scratched him under the chin. "What are we going to do? Huh, Chester? I guess you don't know, either."

Tubby came barreling into the room and jumped up on the sofa next to me. "I know *you* haven't got a clue, Tub-man."

I sighed and closed my eyes. I pictured my brain filled with orange slime. "Ewwwww!" I cried out. Chester jumped off my lap. Tubby just thumped his tail.

I have to stop the ooze. I can't just sit here all night and let myself get dumber and dumber.

I know! I leaped up from the couch. I'll read the manual that came with the chemistry set. Maybe it would have some answers.

I really didn't want to go back in the basement—at least not alone. So I made Tubby come with me. I didn't even glance at the cooler. I just grabbed the manual out of the box and ran back upstairs.

I raced to my room and slammed the door behind me. Then I sat down at my desk and turned on my reading lamp. Tubby plopped down at my feet.

You can do this, I told myself. I opened the manual to the first page.

"Oh, no!" I groaned. The words were so hard. "Compounds. Elements. Neutralize." How was I supposed to understand big words like that?

Miss Scott would say to look them up in the dictionary. She was always making us look up words.

I pulled my dictionary off the shelf and flipped to the words beginning with the letter *C*.

I ran my finger down each page. "Com," I muttered. "Com-p. Com-p-oun-d."

Found it. "Composed of or resulting from union of separate elements, ingredients, or parts."

"What does that mean?" I wailed. Okay, okay, don't give up, I told myself. Start with a smaller word.

I flipped to the words beginning with the letter *P*. "Parts," I mumbled. "Parts, parts, parts."

Here it is. "One of the often indefinite or unequal subdivisions . . ."

I slammed the dictionary shut and pounded my head on my desk.

"This is hopeless!" I shouted. "I'm stupid. I'm just too stupid."

Then I had a horrible thought.

How dumb would I be tomorrow?

10

The next morning I didn't have to wonder why I felt so weird. I knew what was wrong. I knew I was dumber. But that was about all I knew.

If I took everything slowly—and didn't say much—I figured I could make it through the day without doing anything too stupid.

I managed to put on jeans and a shirt and my socks. Now came the hard part. My shoes.

I picked up one shoe, flipped it upside down, and studied it. Then I studied my feet. I found a match!

I slipped my shoe on. It felt comfortable.

I didn't even have to think about the other shoe. I stuck it on the other foot and I was set.

You are doing good, I told myself. Very good.

Now I had to brush my teeth and comb my hair. I headed into the bathroom.

I just needed three things—a comb, a toothbrush, and toothpaste. Simple, right?

Well, sort of. It didn't take too long to wash the toothpaste out of my hair.

I rinsed the toothpaste off my comb, put some on my toothbrush, and brushed my teeth.

I didn't bother eating breakfast. I wanted some extra time—in case I got lost on the way to school.

Mom handed me the plastic container with my lunch in it as I headed past her.

"Your dad and I talked about you and the chemistry set last night," she said.

Great, I thought. I have enough to deal with today without a lecture from Mom.

"It was irresponsible of you to use that set without the safety lesson," she told me. "But we know how hard you've been working lately to prepare for the Science Bowl. So we have decided to let you off this time."

Whew! That wasn't bad at all.

"Thanks, Mom," I called. Then I headed out the front door. Concentrating on each step I took, I managed to reach the school before the first bell.

"Hey, Brains!" someone yelled.

I turned and spotted Eric leaning against the big

oak tree in front of school. "Oooooh," I moaned. I had forgotten about Eric.

"You're lucky I didn't find you after school yesterday," he growled.

"Yeah," I muttered, and kept walking.

Eric circled around me and blocked my way. He shoved a piece of paper into my hands.

"What's this?" I asked.

"My math homework," he said. "It's due this afternoon."

"Do you want me to help you with it?" I asked.

"Noooo," Eric crooned. "I want you to do it. And I want it done by lunch!" Then he strutted up the school steps.

I stared down at the paper.

"And do yourself a favor, Sterner," he called back to me.

"What?"

"Do it right," he snarled. "No funny stuff like yesterday. This is your last chance!"

I glanced down at the paper again. I felt my head start to hurt.

Numbers. Lots of them. With math you have to expect that.

But the paper also had tons of strange little symbols on it. They looked familiar. But none of them made any sense to me.

I had to find Colin right away. He knew what was going on. He would help me.

56

I ran up the front steps, through the double doors, and down the hall. If I reached Miss Scott's room before the final bell rang, I could explain everything to Colin. Then he would do Eric's homework for me! I knew he would!

"Ready for tomorrow?" someone called. Alix trotted up beside me with a big grin on her face.

"Tomorrow?" I asked. "What's tomorrow?"

"As if you didn't know," she teased. "I bet you have been studying for the Science Bowl nonstop. Admit it, Al. You don't want everyone around here to say your sister is smarter than you are."

"I guess not," I mumbled. "I guess not."

The bell rang as soon as we walked through the door. Miss Scott started the class immediately.

No time to talk to Colin.

Now what was I going to do?

Eric was expecting his math homework at lunch. And I wouldn't be able to talk to Colin before then.

I guess I'll have to try it by myself, I thought. I stared down at the assignment. Studying it as hard as I could.

What did that little cross mean? And what was that line with the dot above and below it?

I could feel Eric's hot breath on the back of my neck. I'll never figure this out. Never. He's going to kill me.

The hours until lunch passed so quickly—I could hardly believe it when the bell rang. "I'll be waiting right outside the door for my homework, Brains!" Eric growled.

I carefully returned my books to my backpack. I gathered all my pens together and put a rubber band around them. I organized my pencils, then I brushed the pink fuzz off my big eraser.

How long would Eric wait for me? Would he give up and go to lunch? Or would he guard the door until I got there?

"Al?" Miss Scott asked. "Aren't you hungry?"

I glanced around the room. All the other kids were gone. "Not especially," I said. "Do you know where the sponge is? I want to wash the top of my desk."

"Later, Al," Miss Scott said. "Go to lunch now, even if you aren't hungry. It's an order. Go to lunch."

When I stood up, my legs started to tremble. But I had no choice. I had to walk out that door.

"Hand it over!" Eric barked the second I stepped into the hall.

"I didn't . . ." I mumbled. "I couldn't."

"Wrong answer, Al-vin." Before I could say another word, he lunged at me.

He grabbed the back of my shirt, but I jerked free. I took off toward the cafeteria. When I reached the double doors, I spun right and ran down another hall.

A group of fifth graders swarmed down the stairs. I pushed my way into the crowd, taking the stairs two and three at a time.

"Hey, use the other stairs!" one of the kids shouted.

"Don't you know this is the down staircase?" another kid yelled. "What are you, a moron?"

I didn't bother to answer.

I plowed through those kids all the way to the next floor.

I glanced over my shoulder. Eric stood at the bottom of the stairway, trying to fight his way up.

"I'm coming for you, Sterner!" he shouted.

I bolted down the hall until I came to another staircase. It was the up staircase, but I ran down it as fast as I could. Before anybody could stop me, I raced straight out of the school.

I didn't stop running until I reached home. Mom and Dad were both at work. Michelle was still in school.

What am I going to do? I thought. What am I going to do? I have to figure out something.

But I can't, I realized. I just can't. I couldn't even do a simple math problem anymore. How could I figure out what to do about the ooze—a much bigger problem. Much bigger.

There was no way I could.

I was just too dumb.

And getting dumber every second.

11

"**A**l! Wake up!" Dad called. "It's Science Bowl day!"

I didn't want to wake up. I didn't want to go to school. And I definitely didn't want to be in the Science Bowl.

I rolled onto my stomach and buried my head under my pillow.

I heard Dad open my door. "Al, get moving. Do you know what time it is?"

I opened my eyes and stared at the alarm clock. The little hand was on the seven and the big hand was on the two.

But what did that mean?

I couldn't remember how to tell time.

I sat up, rubbed my eyes, and stared at the clock

again. I still had no idea what it said. How could I forget something I learned back in kindergarten? I was stupider than ever!

Dad walked over and sat down on the bed next to me. "Better step on it, Al. You need to be sharp if you expect to shine at the Science Bowl this afternoon!"

"But, Dad, I really don't feel . . ." I began.

But he wasn't listening. "You need to have a good breakfast. That's very important. And you need to find a few minutes before the Science Bowl to give yourself a mental pep talk," Dad instructed.

"Mmm-hmm," I mumbled.

"I know you'll do great. Just like your sister!" Dad clapped me on the back and left the room.

I thought I was doing great when I was able to get dressed, brush my teeth, and comb my hair with no mistakes. But I knew it would take a lot more than that to please Dad.

I shuffled into the kitchen and plopped down in my chair.

Michelle grinned her horrible grin at me. "Ready for the big day?" she chirped.

I grunted. What could I say?

My mom set a plate of scrambled eggs and bacon down in front of me. "Protein is good brain food," she said.

I knew I needed a lot more than protein to get through the Science Bowl—without the whole school laughing at me. I needed a miracle.

"Let me quiz you," Michelle suggested. She picked up my *Science Teasers* book.

"You mind if I eat first?" I grumbled.

"I'm trying to help you build up your confidence." Michelle pouted. "It's how *I* won all the Science Bowls *I* was ever in."

Michelle thumbed through the book. "We'll start with an easy one. Here's an astronomy question. What was Galileo's earth-shaking discovery?"

I had no idea.

I shoveled a huge forkful of scrambled egg into my mouth, hoping I would come up with an answer before I swallowed.

I didn't.

"Come on, Al," Dad urged. "Just give her the answer."

"I'm hungry," I complained. "I don't want to be quizzed now."

"I was only trying to help," Michelle whined.

Mom ruffled my hair. I hate that. It makes me feel like such a baby. "He's probably nervous. It's his first Science Bowl, after all."

"I'll give you a hint," Dad said. "It has to do with what you are to me."

I spooned some jelly on my toast and took a huge bite. Think, I told myself with each chew. Think, think, think. What was I to Dad? His kid. What could that have to do with Galileo?

"Now I'll give you a hint," Michelle volunteered. "It doesn't have to do with what I am to Dad."

Michelle's hint only made me more confused. Why wouldn't they leave me alone?

"You can do it, *son*," Dad said.

I tried to smile at him. But I had no idea what the answer was. Galileo. Galileo. It sounded like the name of one of those Teenage Mutant Ninja Turtles.

"The *sun* sure is bright today," Michelle said. "I love the *sun*. Don't you, Al?"

I drank my whole glass of orange juice without taking a breath. But when I set my glass down, Mom, Dad, and Michelle were staring at me. Waiting for my answer.

Michelle shook her head in disgust and shoved *Science Teasers* back over to me. "Galileo's earth-shaking discovery was that the earth revolves around the *sun*." She said each word slowly and clearly.

I pretended not to hear her. I pretended to study *Science Teasers* so my family would lay off. But I could only understand a couple of words on every page.

"You want to make Mom and Dad proud, don't you?" Michelle asked. She never gives up. "And don't forget Mr. Gosling. You want him to be proud, too, don't you?"

Mr. Gosling was my science teacher. I felt my head start to throb. What Michelle said made me think of something. Something important. But what?

Mr. Gosling, I thought. Something about Mr. Gosling.

What do I know about him? Not much. He's smart. I know that, I thought.

That's it. *He* is smart. *He* isn't getting stupider and stupider. If I show the ooze to him, maybe he can help me!

I finished the rest of my breakfast as fast as I could. I stuck my plate and orange juice glass in the dishwasher, but I stuck my spoon in my pocket.

I spotted the plastic container Mom kept her coupons in on the counter. Perfect. When no one was looking, I emptied the coupons into a drawer and stuck the container under my shirt.

"Be right back," I announced. "I left my notebook in the basement."

The cooler was still under the table, just where I left it. I opened the lid. Only a crack. I couldn't let the ooze splash me—the way it did the day before. I couldn't afford to get any stupider.

I peeked into the cooler. Whoa! The ooze had grown. And it had more veins. Lots more throbbing veins.

My heart pounded as I stared at the disgusting glob.

I started to jab the spoon in—but the ooze jerked away from it. It moved from the spoon—before the spoon even touched it.

I slammed down the lid and jumped back in fear.

This stuff was disgusting *and* creepy. Totally creepy.

My hands started to tremble as I inched toward the cooler again. Don't think about it, I told myself. Just scoop some up. All you need is a little bit on the spoon.

I opened the lid again, shoved the spoon deep into the quivering mass, and dropped a blob of it into the container.

I clamped the lid on and made sure it was sealed tightly. Then I smuggled the ooze back upstairs and slid it into my backpack.

"Wish me luck," I said as I slipped the backpack over my shoulder.

"Good luck." Michelle laughed. "You're really going to need it!"

Mom gave me a hug and my plastic lunch container with a sandwich inside. "Good luck, Al!"

Dad shook my hand. "We'll be in the audience cheering you on!" he said.

I nodded. And as I walked to school, I tried not to think about my parents . . . watching me in horror . . . as I gave one wrong answer after another in the Science Bowl.

Alix and Colin were waiting for me on the school steps. "You ready for the big day, Al?" Alix asked.

"I studied for it," I said. That was true. And it was better than telling Alix she now had an idiot for a Science Bowl partner.

"I'm betting on both of you!" Colin told us as we headed toward Miss Scott's class.

Eric was already there when we walked through the door. And he did not look happy.

I carefully slid my backpack under my seat and pretended not to notice him.

"I flunked the math homework," Eric told me. "You know what that means?"

I shrugged.

He poked me in the back. "That means I had to stay after school again. And you know what that means?"

I shook my head. Why was he asking me so many questions?

He poked me in the back again. "That means I had to miss baseball practice again. No one makes me miss practice and gets away with it, Sterner! No one." Poke. Poke. Poke.

"I couldn't figure out the problems, okay?" I blurted out. "I'm not smart enough."

"Oh, yeah. Right," Eric shot back. "I'm going to get you, Brains. You can count on it. . . ."

Wrong, Eric, I thought. I don't know how to count anymore.

Eric would have gone on and on, but Miss Scott

entered the room. She paused by my desk. "Are you feeling better today, Al?"

Huh? Why was she asking me that? She didn't know about the ooze. Did she?

"You left school early yesterday," she reminded me when I didn't answer. "I hope you're feeling well enough for the Science Bowl this afternoon."

Oh, yeah, I thought. I did leave early yesterday. "I'm okay," I mumbled.

Miss Scott continued up to her desk. "You aren't going to be okay when the lunch bell rings," Eric whispered. "When I catch up with you, you are going to be very dead meat."

I didn't bother trying to follow Miss Scott's social studies lesson. Or the grammar lesson after that. I just kept my eyes focused on the top of my desk and hoped she wouldn't call on me.

Eric never let me forget for a second that he was going to get me. He dropped his pencil next to my desk and muttered "meat" when he bent down to pick it up. He threw a tiny note over my shoulder that said *very* dead meat."

The morning crawled by. But finally it was almost lunchtime.

At least I thought it was. The big hand and the little hand of the clock were both straight up.

"Who can tell me what the direct object is in this sentence?" Miss Scott pointed to the chalkboard.

Don't look at her. Don't move a muscle, I told myself.

"Al?" Miss Scott called.

"Al?" Miss Scott said again. "The direct object?"

Eric snickered.

I felt my hands start to sweat. My throat tightened up.

Then the intercom crackled. "Will the contestants in this afternoon's Science Bowl please meet in the library," the school secretary said over the speaker. "Mr. Emerson would like to have a brief meeting with you before lunch."

Saved! At least for now. I grabbed my backpack and hurried out of the room with Alix and Toad.

The other Science Bowl kids—Melanie, Tanya, and Geoff—met us in the hall.

Mr. Emerson kept us in the library for only a few minutes. He went over the rules of the Science Bowl and told us we were all winners just for competing.

Tell that to my parents, I thought. Or Michelle.

The six of us trooped down to the cafeteria together. "Let's sit at the same table," Alix suggested. We didn't usually eat with each other, but today everyone seemed to feel like it.

I know I did. Even Eric wouldn't try to drag me away from five other kids. At least I hoped he wouldn't.

"I'm too nervous to eat," Tanya said as she sat down next to me.

What does she have to be nervous about? I
thought. She doesn't have ooze for brains.

"Not me!" Alix insisted. "Al and I are ready. You
guys better watch out."

Yeah, right. Poor Alix. It's not fair that she's stuck
with me for a partner. Poor Alix.

I pulled out my lunch and opened the plastic
container.

"No way you guys are going to win," Geoff shot
back. "Toad and I had a three-day study marathon.
Friday, Saturday, Sunday. He slept over and we
quizzed each other nonstop."

"What's that?" Toad asked me.

"What?" I asked. Then I looked down and gasped
I opened the wrong container. It wasn't my lunch
container. It was the container with the ooze.

And the little spoonful I plopped in this morning
had grown. It filled every inch of the container now.

"Let me see," Alix said.

"No!" I shouted. "No," I repeated more softly. "I
mean it isn't food. It's . . . it's . . . nothing."

"It looks like something to me," Alix teased.

I shoved the lid on the container and tried to stuff it
in my backpack.

But Alix was too fast.

She lunged across the table.

She grabbed the container right out of my hands,
ripped off the lid, and plunged her fingers inside.

12

"**N**oooo!" I shrieked. "Nooooo!"

"Hey, I'm your partner!" Alix said. "You have to share with me. I love this Super Slime stuff. My sister got some for Christmas."

I tried to wrestle the ooze from her. But she held it over her head. "I want to play with it, Al. Pleeease."

She grabbed a handful of the orange gunk.

"I want some, too!" Geoff grabbed the container from Alix and scooped out some more.

"Give it back, guys," I begged. "Please give it back!" But no one paid attention to me.

"Hey, don't forget about the Green Team. Melanie and I want some slime!" Tanya cried.

Geoff tossed the container to Tanya. She shoved both hands into the ooze and made a ball.

"Tanya! Give it to me!" I shouted. "You don't know what that stuff is!"

"Of course we know what it is," Melanie declared. "I want some, too."

Tanya slid the ooze over to Melanie. She pulled out a handful. "Want some, Toad?"

"Yeah!" Toad answered.

"Please. Please. Please. Give it to me!" I wailed.

"Sure," Geoff said. He threw a wad of the ooze at me. But he missed, and it hit Tanya right in the forehead.

Tanya loaded her plastic spoon with a mound of the stuff. She bent the spoon backward, then let it go—launching a gob at Geoff. Splat! A direct hit.

"This stuff is so cool!" Tanya exclaimed. "And I love the color. I've never seen this color before. I bet it glows in the dark."

"Give it back," I chanted. "Give it back. Give it back. Give it back."

Toad gave a huge fake sneeze—and pretended that a big gob of ooze flew out of his nose.

"Gross!" Alix yelled.

"That's not gross," Toad said. "This is gross!" He rubbed some of the ooze in Geoff's hair.

Melanie pointed at Geoff's hair and started giggling. She giggled so hard she couldn't talk. Then everyone threw some ooze at Melanie. Everyone except me, of course.

I stared around the table. It was an all-out ooze fight.

Globs of the neon stuff ran down their foreheads and their cheeks. Clumps of it nested in their hair and stuck to their hands.

It was hopeless. Totally hopeless.

They were all going to turn as dumb as I was!

13

"**W**hy won't anyone talk to me?" I asked Alix.

"Because you made such a big deal about the slime. Next time don't be so selfish," Alix said as we headed toward the auditorium. "Then you won't make anyone mad. It's as simple as two plus two equals . . ."

I stopped and faced her. "Equals what?" I asked. "Equals what, Alix?"

I still knew the answer to two plus two. But did Alix? How stupid had the ooze made her?

"Two plus two," Alix mumbled. She frowned. "Two plus two . . ."

You can do it, Alix, I thought. Come on. Two plus two equals twenty-two. You know this.

"What is two plus two?" I repeated.

Alix giggled. "I can't remember. I must be too nervous about the Science Bowl." She smiled at me. "Don't worry, partner," she said. "I'll be fine once it starts."

But I knew the truth. Alix wouldn't be fine. The ooze had definitely drenched her brain.

As we continued down the corridor, I spotted my mom and dad outside the auditorium.

"We wanted to say good luck, honey," Mom called, "before the Bowl starts."

I tried to smile as we walked up to my parents, but I was having a hard enough time breathing.

"Good luck, son," Dad said, slapping me on the shoulder.

"Thanks, Dad," I said. "Thanks."

I peeked into the auditorium. Almost every seat was taken. My throat went dry.

"Let's go," Alix urged. "It's about to begin."

"I know you won't let us down," Mom said.

I waved to my mom and dad and followed Alix into the auditorium. Toad grinned at me as we climbed up onto the stage. "You are going to lose," he mouthed. But Geoff looked a little nervous.

Alix and I sat down at the empty table. I glanced over at Melanie and Tanya. Neither of them appeared nervous at all.

Melanie was blowing a huge, pink, bubble-gum

bubble. Tanya was staring at it as it grew bigger and bigger.

Mr. Emerson stepped out onstage just as Melanie's bubble popped. He glared at her as she pulled pieces of gum off her face.

"Welcome to the first round of this year's Science Bowl!" Mr. Emerson announced. "I want to welcome the students, the faculty, the friends, and the families in our audience. I also want to congratulate our contestants in advance. No matter what happens today, they are all winners!"

I doubted Mr. Emerson would still feel that way when the Science Bowl was over. I knew my family wouldn't.

"Let's start," Mr. Emerson said. "Remember— when one team misses a question, the other teams get a chance at it. Good luck to all of you."

He smiled broadly and took a wad of index cards from his pocket. "We'll start with the Blue Team," he announced.

Whew! At least my team didn't get the first question. "With all the talk about genes these days," Mr. Emerson read, "tell us what the letters in DNA stand for."

Geoff stared at Toad. Toad stared at Geoff.

"Well, don't both jump in at once," Mr. Emerson said, laughing.

How dumb were Toad and Geoff now? Would one of them be able to get the right answer?

"DNA?" Toad asked. "You better take it, Geoff."

"No," Geoff whispered. "You take it. You're always bragging about how smart you are. So prove it."

Toad shook his head. "It wouldn't be fair for me to answer *all* the questions."

Reluctantly Geoff stood up. "DNA," he mumbled. "That's a hard one."

"I'll give you a hint," Mr. Emerson said. "It has to do with genetics."

Geoff stared at the floor. "It sounds familiar." He sighed. "I heard about genetics *somewhere.*"

Why did I have to bring the ooze to school with me? Why? Why? Why? Geoff's brain was pudding— and it was all my fault!

"I can't remember," Geoff finally admitted.

Mr. Emerson turned to Melanie and Tanya. "Anyone on the Green Team want to take a crack at it?" he asked.

Maybe one of them still had enough brainpower to get the right answer. I knew I didn't.

Melanie pulled a piece of gum off her nose and popped it into her mouth. "I don't think so," she said, chewing her gum nervously.

I noticed my parents in the front row. Dad gave me a big thumbs-up. He probably figures I have it made—now that the other teams missed the question, I realized.

"Red Team?" Mr. Emerson asked. He sounded a little worried.

76

I glanced over at Alix. She was muttering "DNA" over and over—and shaking her head back and forth.

"We don't know, either," I told Mr. Emerson.

Someone in the crowd laughed. I thought it was Eric, but I didn't look. I didn't want to see anyone in the audience—especially my dad. He wouldn't be giving me the thumbs-up now.

"Well, maybe we should move on to a different area of scientific investigation," Mr. Emerson said stiffly.

He pulled another card out of his stack. "This is for the Red Team," Mr. Emerson announced. "What is the definition of *ecology?*"

"I know!" Alix cried. She jumped to her feet.

Maybe the ooze hadn't hurt Alix as much as I thought!

"Wonderful, Alix!" Mr. Emerson exclaimed. "Tell us what ecology is."

The big smile on Alix's face turned into a frown.

"Alix?" Mr. Emerson prompted.

"I knew a second ago," she said, biting her bottom lip.

I could hear people in the audience whispering to each other. And a couple kids laughing.

Alix balled her hands into fists. "I *did* know the answer. I did! I did!"

"You'll have another chance, Alix," Mr. Emerson said. "Science Bowls can be tense, can't they? Now, would the Blue Team like to answer the question?"

Geoff pointed to Toad.

"What was the question again?" Toad asked.

Mr. Emerson sighed. "What is ecology?" he repeated.

Toad stood up with his shoulders back and his head up. "Ecology is how much money people make and what they spend it on," Toad said loudly.

"That is incorrect," Mr. Emerson told him.

"Are you sure?" Toad asked.

"What?" Mr. Emerson asked in disbelief.

"Check the answer!" Toad insisted. "My dad's an ecologist—so I know I got it right!"

"I'm an economist! An economist!" a man yelled from the back of the auditorium.

"Are you sure, Dad?" Toad began. "I thought—"

"Toad!" Mr. Emerson interrupted. "Please sit down. The answer is incorrect."

Mr. Emerson turned to Tanya and Melanie. "Girls?" he asked. "Want to give it a try?"

Melanie twisted her charm bracelet around her wrist. "Isn't Ecology the name of that bear who says 'Only you can prevent forest fires'?"

"No, it is not," Mr. Emerson said. I could see sweat shining on his face. "It is not even close."

"Next question. For the Green Team. What year was Louis Pasteur born?"

"Who?" Tanya asked.

"Huh?" Melanie said.

"Red Team?" Mr. Emerson pulled out a handkerchief and wiped off his forehead while he waited for me and Alix.

Alix shook her head. She brushed the back of her hand across her eyes.

I felt my stomach knot. Was Alix crying? She never cried.

"I'm letting everyone down, aren't I?" Alix exclaimed. "I shouldn't be in the Science Bowl. I'm not smart enough."

"Neither is Geoff," Toad interrupted. "He lost us the DNA question."

"You didn't know the answer, either!" Geoff yelled.

"Did, too!" Toad shot back.

"Did not!" Geoff answered. "And you thought your dad was an ecologist!"

"He is an ecologist!" Toad said.

"Is not!" Geoff growled.

"That is enough!" Mr. Emerson snapped.

"Is, too," I heard Toad whisper.

Melanie and Tanya weren't paying any attention to Toad and Geoff or Alix or Mr. Emerson. Melanie had another huge bubble going. And Tanya started braiding her hair.

"I don't even know what two plus two is!" Alix suddenly cried out. "Something's wrong with me! I let you down, Al! I'm sorry!" Then she ran off the stage.

I leaped up and started after her. "Stop, Alix!" I shouted. "It's not your fault. It's my—"

Mr. Emerson grabbed my arm. "One of the teachers will see to Alix," he told me. "Sit down!"

I sat.

"Let's try another question," Mr. Emerson said in a shaky voice. "This is for the Blue Team. Who discovered that the earth revolves around the sun?"

The sun. That reminded me of something. Breakfast—Michelle quizzing me.

"Toad? Geoff? Do either of you know the answer?"

"I don't want to be on his team anymore!" Geoff blurted out.

"Well, I don't want you on my team!" Toad answered.

"Stop!" Mr. Emerson shouted. He closed his eyes for a long moment. "Stop," he said more quietly. "Would the Green Team like to answer?"

Melanie raised her hand.

"Yes, Melanie!" Mr. Emerson sounded so happy.

"Can I get some more gum? I think better when I'm chewing gum, and I just swallowed mine," Melanie said.

Everyone in the audience laughed. I couldn't wait to get off the stage. I couldn't wait for the Science Bowl to end.

"No, you may not have more gum," Mr. Emerson said firmly. I could see a little muscle twitching near his left eye.

"Then I can't answer the question," Melanie replied.

"Tanya?" Mr. Emerson said.

Tanya jerked her head up. "Huh?"

Mr. Emerson shook his head. "Anyone? Can *any-one* tell me who discovered that the earth rotates around the sun?"

I glanced out into the auditorium. My parents were both nodding and smiling at me.

Wait. Wait. I knew this.

I pressed my hands against the sides of my head. If I pressed hard enough, maybe the answer would come out of my mouth.

Something about my dad? No, something about a Teenage Mutant Ninja Turtle.

"Galileo!" I exclaimed.

A big smile broke out on Mr. Emerson's face. The audience burst into applause. My mom and dad clapped the hardest.

I scored the first point in the Science Bowl!

14

Unfortunately, it was also the *last* point anyone scored in the Science Bowl.

Mr. Emerson asked three more questions—and no one even tried to answer them.

Geoff and Toad got into a shouting match over who was stupider. All Melanie would talk about was gum. And Tanya kept trying out new hairstyles.

Finally Mr. Emerson threw his stack of questions on the floor. "I don't know what's wrong with you!" he cried. "We have always had outstanding students in the Science Bowl! You are all bright kids. Just what kind of stunt are you trying to pull?"

"I studied," Toad protested. "Every night. I knew all this stuff before lunch!"

But Mr. Emerson wouldn't listen. I had never seen him so angry. "The Science Bowl is over," he declared. "This school will not hold another one until the students are able to convince me that they are mature enough to take part."

Most of the kids and teachers and parents filed out of the auditorium quickly and quietly. But my parents waited for me at the edge of the stage.

I walked slowly down the steps and followed them out of the school. I didn't know what to say to them.

None of us spoke until we were a block away from home. Then my father broke the silence. "I don't understand what happened today. You aren't dumb, Al," he said.

"I knew Galileo, didn't I?" I mumbled. "I got more points than anyone else, didn't I?"

"But you should have been able to answer every question," Dad replied.

"I'm disappointed in Al's performance, too," my mother said. "But all the kids had a difficult time this afternoon. It was their first Science Bowl. They were all nervous."

"Michelle did brilliantly in her first Science Bowl," my father pointed out. "A little nervousness gets the juices flowing—as long as you know your stuff. And Al obviously didn't."

We turned into our driveway. "Your father and I have to go back to work," my mother said. "You stay in your room and think about what happened this afternoon. We'll talk about it when we get home."

"We have to make sure this never happens again," my father added. "If you aren't careful, you'll ruin your chances of getting into a good college."

College! I probably wouldn't make it through the sixth grade after what the ooze had done to me.

I watched my parents climb in their cars and drive off. Then I headed up to the house. I turned the doorknob and pulled. The door wouldn't open.

I pulled on it again—as hard as I could. It still wouldn't open.

Then I turned the doorknob and *pushed.* The door flew open and I stumbled inside.

My pulse thudded in my ears. I could hardly remember how to open a door. What was I going to do?

I walked down the hall to my room and sat down on my bed. Tubby wandered in and jumped up next to me.

I noticed a magazine on my nightstand. It had a photo of a pair of in-line skates on the cover. I tried to read the name of the magazine. But after the *S* I gave up and threw the magazine on the floor.

I flopped back on my bed and stared at the ceiling. The ooze had destroyed my life. I couldn't read. I couldn't think clearly. I couldn't open a door.

Mr. Emerson was furious at me. My science teacher, Mr. Gosling, probably felt humiliated.

And my parents—my parents thought I was a total loser.

I didn't even want to think about what Michelle would say to me when she heard how I blew it at the Science Bowl.

But here was the worst thing—four other kids touched the ooze. Their lives would be ruined, too. And it was all my fault.

How stupid were we going to get? I wondered.

I decided I really didn't want to think about it anymore.

I didn't want to think about what else could happen to us before the ooze completely destroyed our brains.

I didn't want to think about it—because I had absolutely no way to stop it.

15

*B*uzz.

I sat up in bed and listened.

Buzz. There it was again.

I should do something when I hear that sound. But what?

Buzz. Buzz. Buzz.

I left my room and followed the noise—to the front door.

"Al, let me in!"

It was Colin.

The doorbell. That's what the buzzing sound was— the doorbell. And when you hear the doorbell, you open the door, I told myself.

I pulled open the front door—on the first try!—and

Colin rushed in. His face was red and sweaty. He must have run all the way from school.

"It was the ooze, wasn't it?" Colin asked, panting.

I nodded. "Everyone in the Science Bowl touched it. Now they're dumb, too."

"What are you going to do?" Colin exclaimed.

"I don't know," I moaned. "I have to find some way to get our brains back. But I'm too stupid to figure out how!"

"Don't worry," Colin said. "I'll help you."

What could Colin do? He was smarter than I was now. But that didn't make him smart enough to solve this problem.

"We have to kill the ooze," Colin declared

"Wait," I said. I knew there was something wrong with that idea. But what? "Wait. If you kill the ooze . . . maybe you would kill our brains with it."

"Oh, yeah," Colin answered. He shut his eyes. His forehead wrinkled as he thought.

Then his eyelids popped open and he smiled. "I have a plan. We have to, um, what's that word? I know I got it right on the science quiz."

"Don't ask me," I told him.

"Neutralize!" Colin burst out. "That's it. We have to *neutralize* the ooze."

"Neutralize?" I repeated. That word sounded familiar. But I had no idea what it meant.

"We find a chemical and add it to the ooze, and then the ooze loses its power," Colin explained.

87

"Maybe if you touch it after we neutralize it, you'll get your brains back. Come on. Let's go down to the basement."

What Colin said seemed to make sense—but, then, what did I know? I was stupid.

"The first thing we'll do is get a little piece of the ooze," Colin said, racing down the basement steps. "Then we can try different chemicals on it until we figure out what will neutralize it."

Colin hurried over to the cooler. He dragged it from under the table. Then he reached for the lid.

"Stop!" I yelled. "Open it only a little," I warned him.

"Okay, okay," he replied. He opened the lid a crack.

Thud-thud. Thud-thud.

What was that? It was a familiar sound, I knew that. One I'd heard a million times.

Thud-thud. Thud-thud.

A heartbeat! That's it! A heartbeat!

But it wasn't my heartbeat.

I broke out into a cold sweat.

I inched up behind Colin. He opened the lid a little wider. I leaned down and peered inside.

Deep in the center of the ooze I saw it. A heart. Bigger than my fist. Much bigger. With tangles of thick twisted veins running through it.

The hideous heart pumped and pumped. The huge veins throbbed with every *thud-thud*.

"A heart!" Colin gasped. "It grew a heart!"

Bam!

Without warning, the ooze exploded out of the cooler in a giant wave. It crashed against the lid, sending it flying across the room.

Colin jerked me back as the quivering orange mass sprang from the cooler. It landed on the floor in front of us with a horrible plop.

Then it started to grow. And grow.

It grew so fast, we could see it happening.

"H-how is it doing that?" Colin stammered.

"I-I don't know," I replied. "But it's not stopping."

The ooze stood at least four feet high now. A big orange mound—shaking and rolling.

We backed up. The ooze shimmied forward.

Does it know we're here? Can it sense us somehow?

I took another step backward and—*screech!* I stepped on Chester. I didn't even know he was down here with us.

Chester raced past me—and headed straight for the ooze.

"Chester, no!" I screamed. "No!"

The cat skidded to a stop inches away from the slime. He whirled around.

But he wasn't fast enough. The ooze rose in another wave. Then it crashed over Chester—and trapped him inside its quivering walls.

I watched in horror as Chester tried to fight his way

89

out. The ooze bulged and stretched as he slammed against it.

One of his claws slashed through the slime. But the ooze quickly sucked it in again.

Then Chester's head broke free. He twisted and jerked, struggling to push his body out of the throbbing trap.

I lunged toward the cat—to try to pull him out.

Colin grabbed my arm. "Don't!" he ordered. "You can't help him. The ooze will get you, too!"

Chester uttered a long wail that made the hair on my arms stand straight up. I could hardly watch as the ooze spread back up over Chester's head. Over his eyes. His nose. His mouth.

Chester gave a last strangled yowl as the ooze let out a horrible slurping sound. Then Chester was gone.

Smothered by the ooze. Totally smothered.

My knees trembled hard. I pressed myself against the wall so I wouldn't collapse.

My eyes remained glued to the quivering mass as it slowly slid across the floor, slithering right by us.

"Hey! Look!" I cried out. "Look!"

The ooze left a slimy trail in front of us. And in the middle of it sat Chester.

It let him go! It let him go! Chester was alive!

"Here, Chester!" I called.

Chester didn't move.

"Come here, kitty-kitty," I urged. "You're okay now."

Chester just sat there. Staring into space with his mouth hanging open. He looked totally out of it— dumbstruck.

Dumbstruck!

"Oh, no!" I moaned when I realized the truth. "Oh, no! Chester's completely dumb. Completely dumb! The ooze sucked out *all* of Chester's brain! *All of it!*"

"Look!" Colin croaked, pointing to the horrible slime.

The ooze had stopped in its tracks.

It began to shake really hard now.

"It's going to explode!" Colin screamed. "It's going to explode! Run! Run!"

But I couldn't run. I couldn't move. I could only stare at the horrible ooze, shaking wildly now and starting to stretch! Stretching straight up. Higher and higher.

My jaw dropped as it grew. I could see its hideous heart, hammering away, as it rose up, taller and taller. Ten feet tall now.

Then, with a sickening *thwack,* two huge bubbles appeared on each side of it.

They began to stretch, too—stretch out. Out to the sides. Out, out, out.

"Wh-what's it doing?" Colin stammered.

"I-I think it's growing arms." I gaped in fear. "It— it is. It's growing arms!"

"Oh, no," Colin croaked. "Hands, too."

Hands. Two wet, glowing hands sprang out from the long, moist arms.

And then we both gasped—as eight fingers grew from each hand. Long, glowing fingers that began to snake out.

Snake toward us.

Reaching. Reaching. Reaching—for our throats.

16

"**N**ooooo!" I screamed. "Nooooo!"

The ooze's glowing fingers stretched until they were inches from my face. Then they stopped.

Colin grabbed my arm and pointed to the creature's body. "I don't think it can move now that it's changed shape," he whispered. "I think it's stuck to the floor."

I stared at the neon-orange body. Colin was right. The bottom of the ooze was rooted to its spot. Its hands couldn't reach any closer.

"Let's get out of here!" I cried. "Now!"

Colin and I edged away from the ooze. I trained my eyes on the creature—careful to stay out of its grasp.

Then I froze in horror.

"L-look, Colin. Look." A round bubble was forming on the top of the ooze. "It—it's growing a head."

My heart pounded as the bubble grew and grew, then tore open in two spots—forming empty, staring eyes.

With another rip a huge hole opened, forming a hideous, gaping mouth.

But the worst part was the brain.

The ooze had a massive brain.

I could see it pushing, pulsating against the top of the creature's head. Straining against its slimy skull.

"Come on!" Colin yanked on my arm. "Let's go!"

But I didn't move.

I stood there—frozen. And watched as the horrible ooze creature began to grow legs.

"Run!" Colin screamed. "Run!" He grabbed my arm and yanked me toward the steps.

We charged up the stairs and into the kitchen.

Squish. Squish.

Oh, no! He's following us. He's following us!

"We have to hide!" I cried. "Hide!"

Squish. Squish.

"It's here!" Colin screamed. "It's here!"

The ooze creature stepped into the kitchen with one of its slimy orange feet.

"This way!" I shouted to Colin.

We raced into the living room and down the hall.

I ran past the linen closet. The linen closet—a good

place to hide, I thought. "I'll hide here!" I told Colin, backing up. "You hide in my room!"

I ducked inside and closed the closet door. I heard Colin race into my room.

I stood in the hot, dark closet, panting. Gasping for air.

Squish. Squish.

He's coming! He's coming down the hall! *Please don't let him find me. Please don't let him find me,* I repeated over and over.

Squish. Squish.

The sickening sounds grew louder—closer.

Squiiish.

The creature slid to a stop—right outside the door.

I grabbed the doorknob with my trembling hands. Ready to bolt.

I waited. But nothing happened.

I listened. Total silence.

What is it doing out there? What?

Why isn't it opening the door? It has hands. It can open the door. Why isn't it doing it?

I pressed my ear against the closet door.

Silence.

Where is it? What is it doing?

I know! It *can't* open the door, I realized. Its hands are too slimy. They're probably slipping right off the doorknob.

Yes! I silently cheered. Yes! It can't get in!

Then I felt it. Something hot and squishy soaking through my socks.

I gazed down—and gasped.

The ooze! It was sliding *under* the door!

And rising higher and higher each second.

I turned the doorknob and pulled. The door was stuck!

I pounded on the door with both fists. I clawed it with my fingernails.

"Open!" I screamed. "Open, open, open!"

The ooze reached my knees now. And it was rising faster and faster. My feet felt as if they were cemented to the floor. I jiggled my legs, trying to keep them moving in the horrible slime.

I grabbed the knob and pulled again. Pulled with all my strength as the ooze bubbled up to my waist. Trapping me in its cold, wet body.

"Open! Open!" I screamed at the door again and again.

And then I remembered—I *pushed* the door, and it swung open, shoving aside a glob of ooze that still remained in the hallway.

With a huge burst of strength I broke out of the slimy mass that surrounded me. I raced to my bedroom.

"Wh-where is it?" Colin stammered from under my desk.

"It's—"

"Here!" Colin finished my sentence.

I spun around.

There it stood, right outside the door—fully formed and bigger than ever. At least twelve feet tall now—with hair!

The creature had grown hair—black wiry hair that sprang out of its entire orange body.

"Oh, gross!" Colin moaned, pushing himself farther under my desk.

The long hairs quivered, quivered madly, as the creature slowly bent his legs and ducked through the doorway.

"No," my voice cracked. "No."

"Its head!" Colin whispered. "Look at its head!"

I stared at the monster's head. It was huge—bigger than a basketball. And an enormous brain bulged out of it. Pulsed against its sides—as if it was way too big for its head.

My heart pounded in my chest as I backed away.

The creature stared at me with its empty eye sockets. Then I watched in horror as its gaping hole of a mouth slowly opened.

"Do not move, human," its deep voice rumbled. "Do not move. There is no escape now."

17

"**L**-leave us alone." I stammered. "Leave us alone."

"Oh, no. It talks, too," I heard Colin croak as the creature oozed forward.

"You have done very well," the creature spoke to me. "You followed the instructions—and you brought me to life. A good plan, don't you agree?"

"I-I don't understand," I stuttered.

"I will explain," the creature replied. "And then I must leave—with your brain."

I knew I didn't want to hear this, but I also knew I had no choice. My whole body trembled as I listened.

"My planet needs human brains," the creature started. "Smart human brains. To give us expanded brain power. The question was—where to find them? Chemistry sets!" the creature exclaimed. "Smart humans use chemistry sets."

The alien creature slid forward. "So we slipped those instructions into chemistry sets all over Earth. And you did the rest. A clever plan—wasn't it?"

The creature didn't wait for an answer. "Enough explaining," it declared. "Now it is time for me to take the rest of your brain."

"Noooo!" I cried out. "No way!"

What should I do? What should I do? Think! Think! I told myself.

And then it came to me. *RUN!*

I dodged around the oozing alien and ran into the hall.

Squish. Squish.

The ooze creature chased after me. Sliding down the hall. Moving fast now. Incredibly fast.

I reached the living room and headed for the front door. *Pull* it open. *Pull* it open, I reminded myself, reaching out for the doorknob.

I twisted the doorknob—and pulled.

The door swung open—yes!

But it was too late.

The ooze shot out a hot, sticky hand and grabbed me.

"Let go of me!" I yelled. The creature lifted me right off my feet. "Let go of me!"

I twisted and turned in the ooze's strong grip.

Tubby charged out of the kitchen—racing in to rescue me!

He ran at the creature. He ran right into him! Right into the sticky ooze.

The creature dropped me as its slimy body wrapped itself around Tubby. "Oh, no! Oh, no!" I cried out. Poor Tubby! He was trapped inside those hideous quivering walls.

I stared in horror as Tubby tried to claw his way out. But it was no use. There was no escape.

And then, suddenly, the creature stiffened. It arched its body, and Tubby came flying out!

He hit the floor with a dull thud.

"Tubby! Tubby!" I scrambled over to my dog. "Are you okay?"

Tubby stared back at me with vacant eyes. The same look Chester had after the ooze sucked out his brain.

"Oh, Tubby," I moaned. "He took your brain. He took your brain."

Squish. Squish.

I jerked my head up. The ooze creature loomed over me.

It was enormous now.

And so was its brain.

I could see it pounding, pounding, pounding against its quivering skull.

"I want the rest of your brain now!" it declared. "I want your brain."

"No!" I shouted. "No! You can't have it. It's mine! It's mine!" I kicked and punched the creature's slimy ooze body. But it was too strong for me.

It lifted me off the floor.

It pulled me up to its awful mouth.

And then, with a horrible slurping sound, it shoved my head down its hot throat.

18

"**L**et me go! Let me go!"

I kicked my legs.

I beat against the creature's slimy body with my fists.

"I'm coming, Al!" I heard Colin shout. "I'm coming!"

I struggled in the creature's hold, and suddenly I felt its grasp weaken. Weaken until it dropped me to the floor.

I watched as it rocked back and forth, moaning in agony.

And then it began to shrivel.

"It's shrinking!" Colin yelled. "It's shrinking! What did you do to it? What did you do?"

"I-I didn't do anything," I stammered.

"You must have," Colin insisted. "You must have done something!"

We stared at the creature as it withered away—growing smaller and smaller. Turning into a formless glob of ooze.

I could still see its brain. But it was the size of a pea.

I could still see its empty eyes.

And there was its mouth. "Look, Colin! Look!" I pointed to the creature. "It's opening its mouth!"

The ooze creature stared up at us.

It opened its mouth.

"Arrf " It barked.

"Whoa! I don't believe it! I don't believe it!" I shouted.

"What? What?" Colin asked.

"Tubby's brain! Tubby's brain took over the ooze. It neutralized it!" I said. "I bet it could live on only smart brains. Tubby's dumb brain must have put him in shock or something. It couldn't handle Tubby's dumb brain!"

I glanced back at Tubby. He seemed exactly the same as always. I guess he didn't use his brain much.

"You were right, Colin. The ooze had to be neutralized. And Tubby's dumb brain did it! It destroyed the creature."

"Wow! Wow! Wow!" Colin couldn't seem to say anything else.

"Hey! Colin! I'm smart again. I'm smart!" I realized. "I got my brain back! And—I *know* what we have to do next!"

"What?" Colin asked, puzzled.

"We have to get rid of it." I jerked my head toward the small puddle of ooze. "We'll stuff it in the cooler and bury it."

"Good idea," Colin agreed. "I'll get the cooler."

I kneeled and tickled Tubby's ears. He rolled onto his back, and I scratched him on the stomach—his favorite spot.

"You saved me, Tub-man," I told him. "If I had a smart pet like Chester, I'd be ooze-food by now."

I guarded the ooze puddle until Colin returned with the cooler and a shovel. We shoveled the puddle into the cooler and slammed the lid on. Then I tied a rope around it, just to make sure the lid stayed on tight.

We dug a deep hole in the backyard—under the apple tree.

Colin and I began to set the cooler into the hole when Colin said, "Wait!"

"What? What's wrong?" I asked.

"What's the capital of Brazil?" he asked.

"Brasilia," I answered, without even thinking.

"Great." Colin grinned. "I just wanted to make sure you were okay."

We dropped the cooler into the hole and covered it up.

We stomped on the dirt until it was hard and flat. And that was the end of the ooze.

19

About a week later everything was back to normal.

Michelle started to teach Chester how to multiply—now that he'd remembered how to add.

I gave up trying to teach Tubby how to fetch. It was hard enough when he *had* a brain. Now it would be impossible. But he's still a great dog.

The other Science Bowl kids all got their brains back, too. We apologized to Mr. Emerson. We blamed our weird behavior on the cafeteria food. We begged him to give us another chance, and he finally agreed.

Which is why I'm stuck outside today studying. I'm spending a great, sunny Saturday afternoon with *Science Teasers* and Mom, Dad, and Michelle. My three coaches.

"Next question, Al," Dad announced. He turned the page of my *Science Teasers* book. "What was Galileo's earth-shaking discovery?"

"I'm sure you know the answer to that one, *son,*" Mom said with a laugh.

While I pretended to think, Michelle wandered over to the apple tree.

"What do you suppose these little orange drops are?" she asked as she gazed at the ground.

I felt my stomach clench as Mom wandered over to the tree. "I've never seen anything like them! They almost glow!" she exclaimed.

"Maybe it's some sort of pollution in the water table," Michelle suggested. "I wonder if they feel as sticky as they look."

She reached out her hand to touch one.

"Don't!" I shouted. "Don't go near it! It could be toxic or something."

"Al's probably right," Mom said, stepping back.

"I don't take advice from inferior life-forms," Michelle declared.

Then she reached down and rubbed one of the orange drops between her fingers.

See? Didn't I tell you that Michelle was just a little too smart for her own good?

Are you ready for another walk
down Fear Street?
Turn the page for a terrifying
sneak preview.

R·L·STINE'S
GHOSTS OF FEAR STREET® #9

REVENGE OF THE
SHADOW PEOPLE

Coming mid-May 1996

Mom smiled, then stood up and headed for the door. "Sleep well," she said, and flicked off the light.

I watched her leave the room.

I heard her gently shut my door.

The room instantly darkened.

I gulped and glanced up at the ceiling.

The same ceiling I saw every night. No shadow.

Then why did I feel someone—or something— was watching me?

I quickly felt under my bed for my silver Eveready flashlight. I keep it there for late-night reading under the covers.

I flicked on the flashlight. The beam of light caught the ceiling. My dresser. My closet.

Nothing unusual. Still, I had that creepy feeling—as if a pair of staring eyes were stalking me.

I clicked off the flashlight. Then I clicked it on again. Having it on made me feel better.

I clutched it to my chest and sat up in bed. I slid up against my headboard, my knees pressed to my chest. I pointed the beam of light out in front of me.

The clock on my dresser said midnight. I felt sleepy, but I couldn't close my eyes. I couldn't stop thinking about that big, black claw reaching for my throat. And now that I was all alone again, it seemed more real than ever. I shivered and pulled the comforter up to my chin.

I stared up at the ceiling.

The head, the horns, the snapping jaw, the shadowy body taking shape on my ceiling. I had seen it. I had no doubts.

I knew that the shadow monster on my ceiling was real.

And I knew it was still there. Somewhere.

And I knew something else.

I knew it was after me.

Brrring!

The noise shot straight through my brain. I bolted up in bed, lost my balance, and hit my head against my headboard.

I rubbed the sore spot with one hand and shut off

the ringing alarm clock with the other. Then I flopped back down on my pillow.

"Yeow!"

I banged my head against the flashlight. Now both sides of my head ached.

What a day. And I wasn't even out of bed yet.

I picked up the flashlight, trying to remember why I had slept with it.

The shadow!

My eyes shot up to the ceiling. Rays of sunlight streaming in from the window lit up the constellations of star stickers there and made them sparkle.

No shadow.

I sighed with relief—until I glanced at my clock. And groaned. I'd gotten only three hours of sleep last night.

I dragged myself out of bed and stumbled into the bathroom. I felt so tired I could hardly push my legs into my jeans. It took all my strength to pull my T-shirt and sweater over my head.

Down in the kitchen I swallowed a few spoonfuls of cereal, then headed for school.

When the bell rang, I sat at my desk, my head propped up in my hand. Mr. Ridgely waddled in and stood at the front of the room.

"Good morning, people," he greeted us in his droning voice. "Let's go over last night's reading assignment."

I opened my book and stared down at the page. I tried to focus on the words, but they swam in front of my eyes.

My eyelids began to droop. My head began to nod. *Bang!*

I shot up in my seat. My heart thudded in my chest.

Two rows over I spied Bobby bending down to pick up his textbook. "Sorry," he muttered.

I thought Bobby's scare would keep me awake for a while, but it didn't. My eyelids felt like two twenty-pound weights. I couldn't keep them open.

I tried pinching myself whenever they began to close. It worked, but only for a few seconds.

Finally, I sat up straight. I stared wide-eyed at my textbook. *Concentrate! Concentrate!* I ordered myself.

The next thing I knew, I felt a trickle of drool drip down the side of my chin.

And something hit me in the head.

I bolted up. Blinked my eyes. I heard everyone laughing.

I spotted the chalkboard eraser on the floor next to me.

Mr. Ridgely stood at the front of the room, arms crossed, staring.

"Sorry to wake you up, Vinny. Have a nice nap?" he asked.

I opened my mouth to answer—and yawned. Which made everyone laugh even more.

"Do you have the answer, Mr. Salvo?" Mr. Ridgely asked stiffly.

Everyone in the classroom grew silent. "Answer?" I chuckled nervously. I didn't even know what the question was.

I glanced at the chalkboard. There were numbers scrawled across it. We were doing math.

I peered over at Bobby for a clue. He shrugged his shoulders.

I was toast.

"Vinny, I'm waiting," Mr. Ridgely said, sneering. "The whole class is waiting. What is the answer?"

I gulped.

"Four?" I squeaked.

Mr. Ridgely's sneer faded from his face. "That is correct, Mr. Salvo. I apologize. I thought you weren't paying attention."

Whew! What a lucky guess.

When Ridgely turned back to the chalkboard, I glanced at Bobby again. He wiped his hand across his forehead and mouthed "How did you do that?"

I didn't know how I did it—but I did know I wouldn't be that lucky again. Which definitely kept me awake for the rest of the morning.

An hour later, a voice boomed over the loudspeaker system. It was our principal, Mr. Emerson.

"Attention, teachers and students. We will now all proceed to the auditorium for the Art Fair awards!"

"Please, please make a double line," Mr. Ridgely ordered.

The class formed two lines and shuffled down the hall.

As I stepped into the auditorium Sharon tapped me on the arm. I barely recognized her.

"What are you doing wearing a dress?" I asked. Sharon usually wears pants and a vest with pockets. She says it makes her look like a real photographer.

"For the art awards today," she answered, tugging at her hem. "I wanted to look nice."

"Oh," I yawned. Sharon gabbed away about the awards. I nodded sleepily. Her voice sounded farther and farther away.

"Helloooo. Vinny, are you with me? *Hey, Vin! Wake up!*" My head snapped up. Sharon's nose was about an inch away from mine. She waved her fingers in my face.

"Uh . . . sorry. What did you say?" I asked.

"What is with you today? It's like you're on another planet." Sharon stared into my eyes.

"I didn't sleep much, okay?" I grumbled.

She shrugged and pushed her hair back from her face. "Well, fine. But you don't have to be a major grouch about it."

"Do you mind?" Emily Nicholson shouted from a group of kids behind us. "You're blocking the door."

Sharon wrinkled her nose at Emily. Then she

grabbed my arm and pulled me into the auditorium. "We need to sit near the front."

Sharon dragged me down the aisle, past the rows of worn leather seats. "I want to sit close to the stage. I'm sure my project is going to win."

I was sleepy. But not that sleepy. I locked my knees and screeched to a halt. *"Your* project!" I shouted. "Since when is it *your* project?"

"Try since always," Sharon said matter-of-factly. *"I* was the one who thought of doing a photo collage. *I* was the one who came up with the theme— 'neighborhood garbage.'

"I was the one who took all of the pictures," Sharon went on. *"I* was the one who developed them in my darkroom—"

"Oh, so I didn't do *anything?"* I cut in.

"All you did was glue them to the poster board and frame the picture." Sharon tried to drag me into a seat.

I glared at her. I wouldn't budge.

"Okay. Okay," she gave in. "I mean, *we* are going to win. All right?"

I gave her a "that's better" look and we sat down.

Mr. Emerson stepped up on stage and coughed into the microphone a few times. Then he started one of his long, long speeches. I closed my eyes and dozed off.

". . . And congratulations to all the students who

entered this contest. Everyone did a great job!" Mr. Emerson finished. He started clapping. Sharon nudged me in the side. I clapped, too.

Then Ms. Young, our art teacher, took the stage to give out the awards. The kids she announced marched up to the stage. Ms. Young handed them each a ribbon and a certificate, and Mr. Emerson shook their hand. Then they lined up behind him. Big deal.

"And in the photography category, the award goes to Sharon Lipp and Vinny Salvo," Ms. Young said.

Sharon jumped up from her seat and pumped her fist in the air. "Yes!"

She tugged on her dress and headed up the stage steps. I followed her, but I tripped on the last step and bumped into Mr. Emerson.

"Whoa, there," he said. He grabbed my sweater to keep me from falling off the stage.

The entire auditorium rocked with laughter.

My face felt hot—and I knew it was red. My head down, I followed Sharon as she marched to the podium.

"I thought we would get a trophy, at least," Sharon complained. We took our place at the far end of the line. "I worked so hard."

Before I could argue with her, Mr. Emerson said, "Smile, everyone."

Dustin Crowley, the school photographer, stepped up to take our picture for the school newspaper.

Dustin lifted the camera. "Uh-oh," he muttered. "I

forgot to load the film. Um . . . stay right there. Be right back." Then he raced out of the auditorium.

My eyes began to droop.

My glance fell to the floor—and I gulped.

Something was wrong.

Terribly wrong.

I saw shadows on the floor—six in all.

Six shadows—but only five winners on stage.

I counted the shadows again.

Definitely six.

My heart began to hammer in my chest as I stared at the sixth shadow. The one that didn't belong to anyone.

It shifted on the floor—changing into something that didn't look anything like a kid.

I tore my eyes away. Peered out into the audience.

I took a deep breath and tried not to glance down—but I couldn't help it. I did.

And gasped—as two twisted horns began to take shape. Then pointy teeth in an alligator snout. And big round eyes.

A thin body began to form. With long legs. And arms that ended in sharp claws!

I leaped back.

It was the shadow. The one I had seen in my bedroom!

The shadow started to slide across the stage. Across the shadows of all the winners—heading straight for me.

About R. L. Stine

R. L. Stine, the creator of *Ghosts of Fear Street,* has written almost one hundred scary novels for kids. The *Ghosts of Fear Street* series, like the *Fear Street* series, takes place in Shadyside and centers on the scary events that happen to people on Fear Street.

When he isn't writing, R. L. Stine likes to play pinball on his very own pinball machine and explore New York City with his wife, Jane, and fifteen-year-old son, Matt.